T0355959

VORTEX

VORTEX

GARY T BRIDEAU

VORTEX

This is a work of fiction. All of the characters, names, incidents, organizations, and dialogue in this novel are either the products of the author's imagination or are used fictitiously.

iUniverse books may be ordered through booksellers or by contacting:

iUniverse
1663 Liberty Drive
Bloomington, IN 47403
www.iuniverse.com
844-349-9409

ISBN: 978-1-6632-6580-7 (sc)
ISBN: 978-1-6632-6581-4 (e)

Library of Congress Control Number: 2024916368

Print information available on the last page.

iUniverse rev. date: 08/12/2024

The Omega strick force characters

Sam, *AKA Alpha One,* head of the O-S-F, is five feet six inches tall, has deep red hair, and rugged looking. He works better alone and has a tough time working in a group unless he is the leader, but he can accomplish more alone.

Tippy, AKA Gamma, is A Will-o-the-wisp or a six-foot-tall Sprite from Dicapl. Her mother is Megan, and her father is Agar. She first appeared in Quest, a Journey, where she accidentally stole Bitsy's husband Harry for a mate. She becomes Prince Blue of the Will-of-the-wisp's gal Friday because she handled herself with a giant spider called a Tree Walker.

Moe, *AKA Beta, is a human female with brown hair and eyes. She is five feet two inches tall. She is a* Miss Know It All, tag-along, spirited, poor, and disabled. She comes from around the city of Phoenix, the capital of the planet Pylee. Moe joined the SG-2 squad as Beta and carries the M.C.W., Moe's Cane Weapon. She is energetic, independent, and stubborn.

Debbie, AKA Delta, is a human female and is *Sam* and Dora's adopted daughter. She is a voluptuous woman in her thirties with long brown hair. She first appeared in Vortex and is in the SG-2 squad.

Kimmy, AKA Epsil the strong, Kimmy is friendly, kind, and empathic. Kimmy is a great listener, and their friends often confide in her. She is naturally curious about everyone and everything. Kimmy loves animals, especially dogs, and wants to own a shiba-inu one day. Kimmy loves swimming, being active outdoors, and traveling.

Greg, also known as Zeta or Brave One, is six feet tall and has short, light brown hair and eyes.

Tina, aka Etan *or the Swift*, is 29 and thirty-five inches tall. She claims to be a Sprite from a remote part of the Galaxy. She is energetic and fast and will charge into any situation with the moxie of someone twice her size. She hates big cities and loves roasted frosty nuts.

The Alpha Wing is their spacecraft shaped like a wing.

The M.C.W.: This is only used by Moe, AKA Beta, because it is set to her D.N.A. The M.C.W. fires a wave of pale yellow energy that incinerates everything in its path. Each team member wears a long dark blue cape with a red omega symbol on the back, a broad-brimmed hat, a broad sword, and an energy pistol.

Their portal: is shaped like a red omega symbol.

Other Characters

Will-o-the-wisp: resembles A6 foot Pixie. When an infant Will-o-the-wisp is born, it is snow white, and as it grows older, they change to yellow in their youth. Then, adult woman are red, the men are dark green and the military is blue green. The ruler is always deep blue weather male or female.

Ab: is a tall, thin figure in a white robe, with light orange skin, dark blue oval eyes, and a small slit for a mouth. His full title is, Master Ashdothmpisgah Shechaniah Bashanmhavothmjair. The name Bashanmhavothmjair was taken from Dut 3:17. He is the leader of a planet called Mystera and is suspended between time and space.

Albert: A heavy-set, arrogant individual who used to work at the Institute but was fired for flirting with Thor's wife Rose.

Cathy T. Loganberry: She is five feet, five inches tall, the moral director at the Institute, and she goes on all the undercover missions for Thor. She is also the only one who can beat Rock on the obstacle course and is the creator of Gideon Bear.

Moonbeam Victoria Dakota: AKA Crystal Stone, a female sprite with yellow hair thirty-six inches tall" from the frozen tundra of Dicapl. She has extraordinary powers when she holds onto a person and can tell their emotions. She loves yellow to the point that most of her clothes are yellow. Moonbeam is head of the sprite security and is spiteful and will get even if someone planks a prank on her. Moonbeam Sprite security took over after Mary Bell married and had a baby girl. But Pixy still takes over when Moonbeam can't.

Ruthie Willus: She wears perfume, which gives off a gentle scent of flowers. She is six feet tall with long, silky brown hair and a fair complexion. She loves long, flowery, pale-colored dresses. Her bright blue eyes sparkle when she speaks.

Darrin Duguay: Detective Darrin, a six-foot tall man with brown hair and hazel eyes, lives in Spokane, Washington, Earth, and prefers to live as a bachelor.

Misty: sprite; short brown hair, thirty-six inches tall, dresses modestly, loved to listen to Bach.

Kayli Aubrette: A feisty Sprite, age 25, is twenty-eight inches tall, is from the planet Pylee, and is on the Sprite security.

Mandy: a five-foot-five-inch tall woman with eyes that are a beautiful shade of hazel, framed perfectly by her long, dark eyelashes. Her hair is a gorgeous shade of dark grey, neatly cut to frame her face. Her body is athletic and toned, and she wears a cute red bikini, accentuating her figure. She likes trying new things and exploring different places.

Alex Smashburger: is a tall man with black curly hair and a beard. He is wearing old jeans and a blue plaid shirt.

Jeff Stearns: He is in his thirties and is five feet ten inches tall with medium-length hair. He was born in the city of Odessa 1000 years ago; his brain was put into the body of a Mandroid and has survived through the years.

Tom Marks: A Mandroid, he is in his mid-thirties and was born in Odessa on the planet Pharez, the garden of the Galaxy. He is intelligent and cunning and has been in trouble with the law many times.

Alice Birdson: A Mandroid. She has light brown hair and eyes in her mid-thirties and is quiet and shy. She was born in Odessa, Pharez, the Garden of the Galaxy.

Terrie Joan Ramsey: A Mandroid, she has short black hair and was born in the city of Odessa

Ariana the Mighty: is five feet six inches tall, with long, soft brown, wavy hair, the kind a man would like to run his fingers through. She loves to jog and skinny-dip by herself because she is shy. She loves crafting art and snuggling up to her man to watch a good movie. She loves creating art and spending time snuggling up to her fiancé in front of a warm fire.

Susan Wong: A cute, slender, five-foot-five Asian woman with short black hair who carries a knife and is a master in martial arts. She is close friends with Connie and Mosey,

Victor Wordly: A short, well-built man with dark brown hair who loves to fight, works for the authorities, and walks limp because of an accident.

Alexis O'Brian: is a petite 4"7 woman who is 30 years old, has bright red hair done up in a pixie, and is a jokester.

Tina: is 29 years old and thirty-five inches tall. She claims to be a Sprite from a remote part of the Galaxy. She is energetic and fast and will charge into any situation with the moxie of someone twice her age.

Storyline

Vortex is a story about an evil queen who has a thirst to conquer new worlds. She opens a vortex to another realm and seduces Alex enter the vortex most likely promising Alex a relationship with her. But he becomes the Queens henchman to enslave everyone on the planet Pylee. However, Alex has to battle the Omega strike force and a bunch of little Sprites who will not give up until they have won.

1

The Whispering Woman

Alex Smithburg, a five-foot-nine, thirty-year-old man with short brown hair, muttered to himself, "As much as I hate to do it, I have to pull off the interstate, to find a place to sleep, for the night."

Miles from the nearest house, Alex finally parked in a small commuter parking lot. Later that afternoon, he leaned against his motor home, nursing his Coconut-Hazelnut coffee, and enjoyed the colorful sky as the sun slipped below the horizon. He whispered, "Lord Jesus, Thank You for the sudden influx of money. By Your Grace, I can help others who are less fortunate."

During the night, a horrendous thunderstorm swiftly moved in, flooding the roads. Suddenly, four powerful, galvanic bolts of lightning struck a rock several hundred feet from Alex's motor home within seconds of each other, tearing a hole in the space-time continuum. Two minutes later, a small vortex appeared and grew larger with each passing minute. The powerful lightning strike Jolted Alex from his sleep. Thinking it was nothing, he rolled over and tried to go back to sleep. But he noticed a strong odor of Musk in the bedroom. Thinking he'd better close his aftershave before he had none left, he went to get up and spotted a white mist forming on the ceiling. Alex's eyes widened as the head of a beautiful woman appeared in the mist. She had long, wavy brown hair and red lips. He could hear her whisper his name. Another clap of thunder distracted Alex, and the woman vanished.

That morning, Alex casually strolled around, examining the damage from the storm of the night before. At the back of his motor home, he spotted a woman in her late twenties in a wheelchair huddled under a tall pine tree. As he approached, he inquired, "Excuse me, ma'am. Is there anything I can do to help?"

"What makes you think I need your assistance?" snapped the woman.

"For one, I've seen drowned rats look better than you. Why don't you come inside and dry off, and I'll fix you something hot to drink."

The woman quickly produced a six-inch knife, stuck it in Alex's face, and stated through clenched teeth, "Oh sure! That's all I need to do. So, you can take advantage of me! You think, because I'm disabled, I'm an easy target. Well, think again, Buster!"

Alex's voice softened as he said, "I'm a born-again Christian, and I guarantee I won't hurt you."

"Well, okay," replied the woman, slowly.

Alex positioned the wheelchair in front of the motor home door and asked, "Do you need help?"

"No, I'm fine. I can walk. Now, please hand me the black garbage bag attached to the back of my chair. Thank you and don't even think of coming in!"

Twenty-five minutes later, dry and presentable, the woman opened the door and said, "Oh, I'm Moe, and I threw out that sludge you call coffee and made some green tea for us."

Inside the motorhome, Alex asked, "Do you mind me asking you a few questions? Like, how did you get here in your manual wheelchair? Were you abandoned? Is there someplace I can drop you off, friend or family?" Alex then noticed a Bible sticking out of her purse and asked, "Are you a Christian?"

Avoiding eye contact, Moe hung her head and answered, "Yes, I am. I know I should trust the Lord Jesus more, but it's hard when you've been hurt so many times."

Alex poured themselves a cup of tea, noticed Moe's sorrowful countenance, and said, "Sis, you look like you could use a hug right about now."

"Okay, but no funny stuff." She placed her hands on the arms of the chair for support and pushed. With her wobbly legs, she found the strength to stand and stretched her arms to Alex. Moe began to sob as a calming peace flooded her inner being. She then cried out, "He threw me out of my apartment because I was only a week late with the rent! It's not fair!"

"What happened to all your belongings?"

"He kept them for compensation. I tried to fight it, but he told the judge I held wild parties, but the judge wouldn't listen to me! After the hearing, I wasn't allowed back in my apartment. If it weren't for the fact that I had stashed a few things in an outside garbage can before the hearing, I'd be up a creek without a paddle." Moe then glanced in back of her to make sure the chair was there and said, "Al, I need to sit. My legs will only hold me for so long."

Once seated, Alex inquired, "Why don't you have a power hover chair?

"On my income, Yeah, right! Get real!"

"What about family and friends? Can't they help you?"

Moe paused momentarily, then explained, "Everyone is too busy with their little world to pay attention to me. They have better things to do than have to deal with a disabled person."

"That's not true," replied Alex. You can stay with me until you locate another place. Tell you what. I'll give you the back bedroom. It comes, complete, with its bath."

Smiling, Moe thanked Alex for his generous offer, then stated firmly, "Okay, under one condition, we lay down a set of house rules. One, you never come out of your bedroom in your underwear, and I'll do the same. When I'm washing up, you are to leave the camper until I'm finished. Hugs are to be kept at a bare minimum and we respect each other's privacy. Last of all, I need your prayers, not your pity. The last thing I need is to have someone hovering over me like her mother hen. Oh, one more thing. Please get rid of those hideous curtains."

"I can't help it; they came with the motor home!" replied Alex.

"I don't care. I am not going to sit here and stare at those fashion nightmares for the duration of my stay." Moe then picked up a foot-square piece of different-colored twisted metal off the table and questioned, "What, pray tell, is this?"

"It's modern art. It cost me a bundle."

"What," shouted Moe, "Boy, did they see you coming. The guy most likely picked it up in a junkyard, painted it, and sold it to the first sucker who came along."

"The guy happens to be a famous artist," answered Alex.

"A con artist is more like it if you ask me," replied Moe. Hey, in ten minutes, we eat the noon meal. Do you have any suggestions?"

"Yeah, an Earth delicacy, Hotdogs, and beans."

"Ah, no thanks, meat byproduct isn't what I call nourishing. How about Tofu, some greens, and green tea," suggested Moe.

"Are you kidding?" questioned Alex, "I'd rather eat dog food than that junk."

"How about this? You eat your food, and I'll eat mine?"

At a stalemate over the noon meal, Moe stood up and made her way to the refrigerator. She opened it and rummaged around for a minute, then exclaimed, "You have farm Pylean eggs? Four of these bad boys, some cheese, will make a splendid omelet."

"Alex mulled over the idea and said, "Sounds good, but no green tea."

"You want me to drink that brown sludge? Well, that's okay. Make sure there's plenty of milk to kill the flavor. Thank you."

As Moe was enjoying her meal, she glanced around and questioned, "No offense, brother, but your motor home looks like it was built in the dark ages. No digital storage cube for food, and what possessed you to buy a motor home with wheels? They went out of style decades ago."

"I like the simple life," replied Alex.

"Simple? Why don't you say you were cheap and stingy? Of course, you know you will spend more money in the long run."

"How's that?"

"Every week, you'll have to go to a store, buy the food, and take it home. You must also take into account the cost of energy and the high cost of real food. In the long run, you will have paid double the cost of your motor home in ten years. Then, there's the cost of new tires."

Alex interrupted, "Alright, I get the picture! What were you born with? A calculator for brains? Now, if you will excuse me, I have things to do in my room."

Moe slowly shuffled her way to her room, where she stayed for the rest of the day. After reading the Word that evening, she went to sleep only to be awakened by the strong scent of Musk in her room and muttered, "I wonder if that's Alex trying out a new cheap cologne?" Then, the thought hit her to check on Alex; she dawned her bathrobe and poked her head out her door. At the same time, the same woman had appeared in a cloud of mist in Alex's room. Only this time was her head visible, and her shoulders were down to her waist. She smiled sweetly, hummed a hypnotic tune, and whispered, "Come to me. I am waiting." Glassy-eyed, Alex slowly got out of bed to leave. As soon as Moe saw Alex in his pajama bottom, she screamed, "Alex! What do you think you are doing? Another dumb move like that, and I'm outta here!"

Alex hollered, "Victoria, where are you?" A bewildered Alex shook his head, glanced at Moe, and said, "Oh, I'm sorry. I don't know what I was thinking."

The next morning, Moe dressed in just her long white robe was up early, had the morning meal on the table, and bellowed, "Alex! Come and get it!"

A groggy Alex staggered out of his room with his shirt half-buttoned, his hair a mess, and one shoe on and no pants. Moe growled, "Please go back to your room and make yourself presentable,"

Some five minutes later, Alex emerged from his room dressed in a blue pinstriped shirt and his white BVDs

Moe snapped, "Spiteful, aren't we."

"Look, Miss Bossy. You don't tell me how to dress! Okay."

A determined Moe placed her hand on the table and the back of the bench to assist her in standing. Once on her feet, she maneuvered herself up to Alex, stuck her finger in his face, and bellowed, "I'm going to teach you how to dress properly, even if it kills me."

Alex promptly threw his arms around Moe, passionately kissed her on the lips, then pushed her on the couch to make Love to her. A terrified Moe was able to pulled her knife out of her backpack, stuck it under his chin, and said, "Back off, buster, if you want to live, to see tomorrow." Then pushed Alex off her before he had a chance to do anything.

Moe hobbled outside in the cool morning air, closed her robe, and sat in her wheelchair and cried, then made plans to find another place to stay.

Dressed in his BVDs, Alex rushed outside, knelt in front of Moe, and pleaded, "Will you forgive me? I don't know what I was thinking of. I guess it's these stupid dreams I've been having lately about this beautiful woman that puts my brain in a fog."

Moe somberly and silently stared at Alex for a minute, smiled and said, "By forcing yourself on me is inexcusable and I want an apology from you and promise that you won't do it again."

"I'm sorry I didn't know what I was doing until you stuck me with that knife."

"Who is this Victoria woman? One of your old flames?"

"It's the woman in the dream I've been having."

Moe stared at Alex and said, "I forgive you but because I'm still shaken up over what you tried to do to me, could you assist me in getting dressed?"

"Didn't you say we are to be modest at all times?"

"I did say that, but since you've already seen me naked when you tried to forced yourself on me. So I guess we can take our friendship just a little bit further and see each other in however they want to be dressed."

In Moe's room she laid out her clothes, took off her robe, then set on the edge of the bed with Alex, handed him her undies so he could help her put them on.

Alex stared at Moe, took her in his arms passionately kissing her lips and pushed her down on the bed and forced himself on her.

After, an angry Moe sat up and bellowed, "That Mister was uncalled for," she softened her town then said, "I guess we are now a couple."

"I am sorry again. My mind is still in a fog and didn't know what I was doing,"

Moe smiled sweetly and allowed Alex to curl up with her in the bed for most of the morning. Around eleven-thirty that day, Moe rolled over in bed, gave Alex a long hug and kiss, then said, "I see that you are actually a kind and gentle man with a heart of compassion, and you are someone who loves the Lord as much as I do. So let's repent and we don't do this again until after we are married. Oh and thank you for this morning,"

Alex assisted Moe in getting dressed, and gave her a cup of coffee the way she likes it. Then the two of them took a stroll in the parking lot to get some fresh air. At the end of the parking lot, Moe stood to her feet, put her arms around Alex, kissed his neck saying, "This morning was not how I wanted a relationship with a guy to start but I'll settle for it. She spotted a swirling mass of air at the end of the parking lot. Then maneuvered around trees and rocks with Alex, and came to a six-foot-tall spinning vortex.

Moe questioned, "Alex, what do you think it is? It's not a dust devil. They only last a short while. Here, hand me that large rock, will you please? I want to see something."

Moe then tossed the rock into the vortex to see what would happen. When the rock vanished, she immediately straightened up and remarked, "That was too weird. Let's get outta here and inform someone who can handle this sort of thing."

Alex stood a three-foot log on end and maneuvered into the vortex with the same results. Moe spun around in her wheelchair and bellowed, "I'm outta here!" She stopped, twisted around, and hollered, "Alex my sweet! Come on, let's go!"

A glassy-eyed Alex slowly turned and walked past Moe. She screeched, "Hey, a little help here!"

Back at the motor home, Moe suggested, "Let's pack and get outta here as fast as we can."

Alex slipped into the driver's seat, but the fusion reactor died.

"You mean we're stuck here?" questioned Moe

"Looks like it. Besides, what's the hurry?" questioned a dazed Alex.

Moe hobbled her way to the back of the motor home and was about to enter her room when the scent of Musk filled the camper. She turned to behold a tall woman, clad in a long, black dress down to her ankles, caressing Alex's face.

Moe screamed, "Get out of here, you foul devil!" Then threw her purse at the woman, causing the image to vanish. Losing her balance, Moe fell to the floor. Determined to help her sweetheart, she crawled up to him and slapped him in the face, saying, "Come on, Alex, snap out of it! I don't care if we have to walk; we're getting out of here."

Alex calmly replied, "No. I don't think so, were staying."

"Well, if you will excuse me. I'm going to read the Word." then struggled to stand. Once in her bedroom, she promptly locked the door. As she stretched out on the bed, Moe opened the Word and began to read. She then found herself walking down a road on a cold, clear winter day, with the presence of the Lord permeating her surroundings. The fields on each side of the road were heavy with snow. Moe felt like a kid, with joy in her heart, as she darted about and exclaimed, "Lord, this place is beautiful. She then pleaded, "Please, Lord! Don't, send me back! I can't do it!"

Everything within her wanted to stay with her Saviour and not have to deal with the trials before her. She heard Christ say, "My child, I know you can do it; I have confidence in you."

Waken from her encounter with Christ, Moe bounced off the bed and out the door, eager to tell Alex about it. When she didn't see him sitting at the table, she knocked on his bedroom door and said, "Alex, are you decent? I've got something I want to share with you." Moe slowly opened the door only to find an empty room. All of a sudden, the word vortex flashed through her mind. Moe spun around on her heels and darted out the door to the end of the parking lot, forgetting all about her disability. Spotting Alex by the swirling mass of air, Moe raced through the woods, hoping to stop him from entering it. Alex smiled at her as he stepped into the vortex and disappeared.

Six feet from the vortex, Moe shrieked, "Alex, No! Don't go in there!" She glanced down at her feet and questioned, "What am I doing? I can't walk, let alone run!" Doubts flooded her mind as her legs suddenly gave way, sending her tumbling to the ground. Feeling powerless to do anything, Moe cried, "Lord Jesus, help me."

Noticing the scent of Musk, Moe glanced up and saw the woman in black standing by her head. "Can you help me up inquired Moe?"

The woman slowly knelt by Moe's side and stated softly, "He's mine now and don't even think of coming after him. Or you'll be the sorriest woman alive. Oh, FYI, the name's Victoria. She stood, laughed, and kicked Moe in the stomach as hard as she could, then vanished with the vortex.

2

The Omega Strike Force

Moe lay helplessly on the ground, gasping for air as she held her stomach, groaning in pain. Then, a soft voice said, "Here, chew these leaves. It'll help ease the pain."

Moe twisted her head and saw a young woman dressed in a light blue slack suit with transparent wings sticking out of her back. She asked, "Are you an Angel?"

"No, I'm Tippy, a Will-o-the-wisp and part of the Omega Strike Force. Here sit up against the tree for a while. Some Wisps scouts spotted this disturbance and reported it to Blue, our leader, who asked My father, the Galaxy Sentinel if I could check it out. Here I am. Can you tell me anything about what has transpired?"

I'm Moe, and my sweet Alex vanished into the vortex because of this evil woman, Victoria. I could have stopped him from entering the vortex, but I doubted the Lord healing my crippled legs and tumbled to the ground before I could reach him."

"Let's get you back to the motor home so you can rest, and then we'll plan a rescue." Tippy stood up, walked up to where the disturbance was, stretched out her hands, and waved them around for thirty seconds, then commented, "This isn't good. There's a rip in the space-time continuum. If it isn't repaired soon, it'll spell disaster for both dimensions.

Grabbing hold of the tree behind her, Moe struggled to stand. Once on her feet, she stated firmly, "In the name of Jesus, I can walk!" With her arms outstretched, she haltingly took a few steps. Then, with confidence, she walked back to the trailer without help.

"You're doing good." remarked Tippy, "Walk out that healing Moe, in the name of Jesus."

At the motor home, Tippy promptly opened the door to enter. But she was stopped abruptly; her wings began to flutter as she hollered, "Whoa, boy the pheromones in here. We need to air this place out, bad. Your boyfriend never had a chance. But don't worry, we'll get him back."

Moe cleared her throat and firmly stated, "I suppose you are wondering why I am living with him. I was kicked out of my apartment with nowhere to go, and Alex gave me a place to stay until I got on my feet, and yes we did mess around on my bed naked once."

"Okay, I'm not judging you. But, if you're feeling convicted about a compromise situation, move out."

"Where?" questioned Moe loudly.

"Jim and Ella, missionaries to the Will-o-the-wisp, would love to have you."

"Could I join them as a missionary and help them?"

"I don't see why not?" answered Tippy. "Now, how about I put on a pot of coffee? It's about that time for the noon meal. Oh, I almost forgot. I've got to call in."

Tippy took out her communicator and called the Institute. "Thor here."

"Hi, Dad. We have a serious situation here. There is a rip in the fabric between the dimensions. The tear is stable for now, but I don't know how long it will last. One other thing. A woman by the name of Victoria lured some man into her dimension."

"I'm sending Debbie as a backup. Do you need your gear?"

"Yes, Dad, and could you send me an extra set about Debbie's size?"

"Give me about ten minutes to get things together."

"Love you, Dad, tell Mom I should be back in time for the Party. Tippy out."

Moe was pouring the coffee when someone hollered from outside, "Hey Tip, you in there?"

"Come on in, Debbie," hollered Tippy.

Seeing a figure draped in a long dark blue cloak and broad-brim hat, Moe screamed, "I'm innocent! It's not my fault! Please don't hurt me!" She then scrunched under the table, trembling.

Tippy knelt, peeked under the table, and asked, "You want to talk about it?"

Concerned, the woman removed her Omega Strike Force garb and stated, "Sorry, I didn't mean to send you into a panic. I guess this outfit can be a little foreboding at times. By the way, my name is Debbie. Tip: your mom sent us a box lunch."

Seated behind the table again, Moe explained, "When I was young, my father would threaten me with a man in a dark blue cape and hat coming and dragging me away and punishing me if I was bad. I'd lay awake at night, afraid that someone was going to crawl in my window and drag me off. I thought I was healed when I received Christ as my Saviour."

"You were healed," Debbie replied. "That's a lie from the devil. Now, let's say Grace and eat."

"What's on the menu?" Tippy asked. I do hope Mom sent us Meatball subs from Earth."

"Earth," questioned Moe, "I've never heard of that restaurant. Is it located on Avalon Prime?"

"It's a planet on the other side of the galaxy, Silly." Tippy handed Moe her foot-long meatball grinder and said, "Here, eat your sub before it gets cold."

Moe stared at the monstrous sandwich and asked, "Did you say sub or club?"

"Sub," replied Tippy.

"Tippy, If you ask me, it looks like the latter. Is there a trick to eating one of these things, or do you start nibbling on it and hope to reach the other side before you're old and wrinkly."

"Cute. Just eat the stupid thing and quit the cryptic remarks, okay?"

After the noon meal, Tippy glanced at her watch and muttered, "I wonder where Dad is with my gear?"

"You mean your cloak, hat, and clothes?" Debbie questioned. "They're over there, on the floor. They appeared a few minutes ago."

Tippy quickly scooped up her stuff and asked, "Moe, do you mind if I use your room to change?"

"No, go ahead."

Tippy tossed Debbie the extra cape and hat and said, "Show Moe how to use it. We'll leave the sword for later."

Moe eagerly put on her new outfit, twirled around, and commented, "How about that? I became what I feared the most! This is so cool!"

I'll make this brief. The cloak has a camouflage energy field and warming circuitry to keep you toasty warm when it's cold out, and it'll deflect multiple energy blasts, too."

Suddenly, a powerful blast of electricity rocked the motor home, sending small amounts of electricity dancing around inside. Tippy raced out of the back bedroom, shouting, "Everyone on the floor! We're under attack! I'll call Dad for backup!"

Debbie peeked out the window at the attackers and muttered, "Tip, I think they're from the other dimension, and the guns they have are really nasty. I don't think our cloaks will repel that type of energy charge."

Debbie dove for the floor as another blast of electricity shattered the window, sending shards of glass flying everywhere.

Moe grumbled, "Are we going to sit here and let them pick us off one by one, or are we going to do something? If we can douse that cannon of theirs with water, we can sort it out."

Debbie leveled her gaze at Tippy, saying, "I thought Will-o-the-wisp were a resilient race. What are you doing, cowering on the floor?"

Tippy glared at Debbie for thirty seconds, then inquired, "Debbie, do you know what will happen to my clothes if I get hit with a charge from their cannon? Then, again, I think you do know. Like when you returned from a mission with your cloak tightly wrapped around you. Humm?"

Debbie's face turned red from embarrassment, and she replied, "I don't want to talk about that subject, thank you."

Moe questioned, "Hey, guys. Do you hear anything?"

"Come to think of it, no," answered Tippy. She poked her head above the counter to look out the window and shouted, "Dad! Were you in here?" Then she darted outside to greet him. Debbie anxiously glanced around and asked, "Is my Dad here?"

"Yeah, he's over by the dimensional tear, taking care of things. He'll be here in a few minutes."

As soon as Sam rounded the back corner of the motor home, Debbie squealed, "Dad!" and then rushed out to meet him.

Feeling left out, Moe hung her head and wandered down the road unnoticed trying to think where she was going to spend the night.

Tippy zipped by Moe overhead and landed ten feet in front of her, with her hands on her hips, glaring at her.

Moe jerked her head up and hollered, "What?"

"Where do you think you're going?"

"To find a place to sleep for the night, if it's any business of yours."

"What about the Vortex?"

"I'm sure you and Debbie can handle things. If you will excuse me, I'll be on my way."

"My father wants to speak to you now."

Moe turned to walk away when Tippy hollered, "Don't you turn your back on me! I said, My Dad wants to talk to you." Tippy took flight, swooped down, grabbed Moe under her arms, then carried her back to the motor home and set her down in front of Thor and Sam.

Thor questioned sharply, "Where do you think you're going, young lady?"

"Alex is gone, the motor home is trashed, and I do not want to be here when more of those creeps make another visit."

Thor glanced at Sam and inquired, "Do you think we should give it to her?"

"I think she can handle the things." Sam then handed Thor a long box. Before opening it, Thor stated to Moe, "Things are getting too rough for Sam and me to handle, and I decided to organize 'The Omega Strike Force.'" Thor handed Moe a cane with a ruby shaft and black handle and said, "This is yours."

Moe cautiously took the cane, then hollered, "Ouch! The stupid thing bit me."

Thor explained, "As part of the Omega team, this will be yours. No one else will be able to use it because of the DNA censor on the handle. It's called M C W and emits a powerful, pale yellow energy wave that will obliterate whatever gets in its way."

Speechless for a minute that The Galaxy Sentinel would pick her to be part of an advanced strike force, Moe finally spoke up and said, "But, I have nothing to offer."

"You have more to offer than you realize. Sam will spearhead the whole operation, and he'll fill you in at Omega's headquarters on Dicapl. Good luck and good hunting. I have to go. I'm taking Rose out to dinner tonight. Sam, keep me informed."

"Will do," replied Sam.

After Thor was transported back to the Institute, Sam asked, "Is everyone ready for the surprise of your lives?"

Moe suddenly interrupted, "Sam, Sir. Is this thing as deadly as you claim it to be?"

"Why don't you try it out on that piece of junk you call a motor home?"

"Wait!" hollered Tippy. "Let me get my things out of there first."

Five minutes later, Tippy placed her belongings in a pile at her feet and said, "Okay, Hotshot, fire away."

Moe grabbed the cane's handle in her right hand, rested the shaft on her left arm, and fired. A wave of pale yellow energy shot out of the end of the cane and enveloped the motor home before it exploded into a ball of fire, turning it to ashes.

Now, that's what I call a weapon!" stated Moe loudly.

At the Omega's base, Sam explained, "Each one of you will be issued a communicator that will have a subspace channel. All Omega communications will be done on that channel. In case of an emergency, each one of you will be contacted over the subspace com line. Your new outfits will consist of a broad-brimmed Black hat and a long, black cloak with a red omega symbol on the back. And a mask, which will cover most of your face. Under no circumstances are you to divulge who you are to anyone. Doing so will mean immediate dismissal from the team. Debbie, you're the pilot of the Alpha Wing. Tippy. "Moe quickly interrupted; excuse me, Sam, Sir, aren't the outfits lacking something? I mean, what do we wear underneath the cape?"

Sam silently glared at Moe and then inquired, "Are you for real?"

Debbie bellowed, "Moe, I said I wasn't going to discuss my coming back from a mission with my long cloak draped around me! Now, drop it!"

Moe snickered and said, "Sorry."

"Without any further interruptions," stated Sam. "The Omega Base is equipped with its own Portal computer. This allows you to go directly to the trouble spot.

"Let's suit up, girls; you have a job. Oh, and I almost forgot about your weapons. Broad swords are out for you three. Instead, you'll have self-generating energy weapons with ruby gun barrels and black onyx handles. The rest you will have to learn as you go along."

Debbie leveled her gaze at Sam and asked, "Dad, where is the Omega Base on Dicapl?"

"Inside the mountain range north of Crystal City." Sam then kissed his daughter goodbye and left.

The Omega Strike Force was dressed in black, ready to tackle their first assignment against the interdimensional queen.

Tippy stated firmly, "We should never go on any mission without praying. Christ first, at all times."

3

The Dragon Queen

"I can't wait to fly the Alpha wing," stated Debbie anxiously.

"You're gonna have to wait for another mission, answered Tippy, "Now, let's suit up and go."

Debbie glared at Tippy and questioned cautiously, "We're not going to be stuck the way we were the last time and had to be rescued by Ab. Because as soon as we destroy the equipment, the rip will automatically seal itself. You know that don't you?"

"Well, then. You'll have to pack an overnight bag in case we have to spend a few years there," quipped Tippy.

A worried expression swiftly appeared on Debbie's face as she slowly inquired, "Are you serious, Tippy?"

"No, now, let's go."

Moe entered the control room, clad in her black Omega outfit, with her cloak wrapped tightly around her legs, and said, "I'm ready."

Debbie furiously marched up to Moe and asked, "Are you looking for a fat lip? You're not going to let it rest until I tell you, aren't you?"

"Nope,"

"Alright! I'll tell you! The stupid slacks I wore were too tight, and I ripped the seat cleanout. There, are you satisfied?"

"Are you?" questioned Moe, smiling.

"Come again?"

"My mother always told me never to hold things inside you. They can fester into something worse."

Debbie began to laugh and then said, "Yeah, I guess it was funny, at that."

Tippy questioned, "Does anyone know how to set up the portal? We Wisps don't do computers."

"One way, or round trip, with a timer?" questioned Moe.

"One way, and set it ten feet from the rift."

in the middle of a grassy meadow, on the other side of the rift, Moe slowly scanned the horizon and inquired, "Tippy, are you sure we're in the other dimension? The scenery looks the same."

"Oh, don't worry about that; we are in the other dimension," affirmed Tippy. "Why? What did you expect?"

"I don't know. Weird sunlight, strange creatures, maybe," commented Moe.

Debbie suddenly whispered, "Shhh, camouflage shields."

Activating their shields, the three women dove for the ground as a large horse-drawn, canvas-covered cart lumbered slowly up to them and stopped. Four men quickly crawled from under the tarp and then pulled it off. The man driving the cart ordered, "Okay, men. Aim the energy cannon directly into the opening and fire a twenty-second burst. That should create a large firestorm to keep those dimensional lowlifes busy until the queen can untie the two dimensions."

Tippy whispered, "Moe, get the M-C-W ready, and we appear on the count of three."

"Already done."

Tippy hollered, "Three!" Suddenly, three black figures appeared, temporarily startling the men. The commander sarcastically asked, "Who do you think you are?"

"We're your worst nightmare," stated Moe as she rested the M-C-W on her left arm, ready to fire.

"Oh?" the commander asked. Are you going to attack me with a cane?" And he began to laugh.

"We are not lowlifes!" shouted Debbie,

"Waste them," shouted the commander.

Suddenly, a wave of yellow energy enveloped the men and energy cannon within seconds, turning them into ashes. That left a stunned commander standing alone. Tippy quickly grabbed the commander and dragged him back through the rift, handing him to Sam for questioning before returning to the group.

"Anyone know where we are headed?" questioned Moe.

"Nope," answered Tippy, "I figure, since those men came from that direction, I think we ought to go that way. I'd fly above the treetops, but I must keep my wings hidden now."

A mile down the road, they heard from the bushes, "Hey, you three. Over here." Then, a thin arm protruded from a large green bush, beckoning them.

"Let's go see what's on the other end of that arm," suggested Tippy.

"Maybe it's a weird, green, smiley monster, with a tong shaped like an arm to lure its prey," quipped Debbie, "Then, with its huge mouth, it'll swallow you whole."

Moe's eyes widened as her heart began to pound. Then, she placed her hand on the M-C-W, ready for action.

Tippy growled, "Debbie! Will you be quiet? Moe, don't worry, there's no creature like that around here."

On the other side of the bush, an old man with a bald head said softly, "Welcome to the land of Tob." He then pointed his bony finger at them and said in a high, squeaky voice, "You came through the opening, didn't you? Come here to attack our queen? That's good. Oh, by the way, you can call me Jether."

"Do you know where the castle is located?" inquired Debbie.

"Her place is well guarded; you will not get within a mile of the place if you will help me with a small favor. I will show you the secret underground passage. Deal?"

The three women whispered amongst themselves whether to accept the old man's offer or try to find the queen on their own when Jether stated, "Your invisible capes won't help you."

Tippy approached the man and said, "Okay, we'll assist you. What is it you want?"

"Follow me, you must,"

The old man led the women through the woods and then across a rope bridge to a village of mud huts. The man pointed to a hut in the middle of the town and stated, "In there, you must go."

When the women had entered the hut, iron bars swiftly slammed shut, sealing them in. Debbie spun around with a jerk and hollered, "Hey, what gives? We came here to help you!"

"Help, yes. As a sacrifice to our god, tomorrow morning, at sunrise."

Moe grabbed Jether by his robe and yanked him to the bars, "You double-crosser!" Then, with the other hand, she quickly reached behind her for her dagger, strapped to her back, and would have stabbed him if it weren't for the guard who tried to ram his spear into Moe's side. You okay, Moe?" asked Debbie,

"Yeah. Another inch, and I would have been dead." Moe leveled her sights at Tippy and inquired, "Can these cloaks repel arrows? Let's make a break for it."

"The capes have never been tested if they are puncture-proof," answered Tippy.

Debbie whispered, "How about if we make a break for it at night?"

"Sounds like a plan," replied Tippy.

That night, while the villagers slept, Tippy approached the barred door and inquired softly, Hey, you guard, "You want to see what I can do? Come closer."

The sentry promptly stepped in front of the door, with his arms folded across his chest, and growled, "Yeah, what?"

"This," shouted Tippy, as she grabbed hold of the bars and shoved. Hit the guard, sending him tumbling to the ground, then she caught him, yanked him up, and landed a right cross to his jaw, knocking him out. Then said, "Come on, let's get outta here." As she wrapped up the guard in the iron bars. On the other side of the rope bridge, Debbie took out her energy pistol and fired, destroying the bridge.

Four miles down the road to the palace, Moe queried, Can we stop for a minute? My side is hurting me."

Tippy quickly glanced around and stated, "We can make camp over there for the rest of the night. "I'll take the first watch."

Around the campfire, Debbie glanced at Moe, who had curled up next to the fire and was asleep. "I think something's wrong with Moe. Tip, can you check her out?"

Tippy touched Moe's side to nudge her and discovered a two-inch gash in her side. "Throw me, my sack, will you, Deb? Moe's hurt."

The following day, Moe felt her side and asked, "When did this happen?"

"Next time, don't try to be Miss Macho," stated Tippy, "You're an important part of this group; remember that the next time you think of doing something stupid."

"What do we do now?" Debbie inquired. "Wait around until she is healed?"

"No, answered Tippy, "I'll scout around for a place where we can set up camp and not be spotted." Tippy stood up, removed her cape and hat, flew straight into the air, and was out of sight in seconds.

Debbie glared at Moe for five minutes, then said, "Thanks a lot, Bone Head! Next time, try to keep your cool."

"Okay, I'll lie down next time and play dead like a good puppy dog."

"You know what I'm talking about!" growled Debbie.

"I did manage to get this." Moe pulled a folded paper out from her inside pocket.

"What's that, his grocery list?" Debbie questioned sarcastically.

Upon unfolding the paper, Moe held it and smiled, "No, a map."

"Of what?" inquired a wide-eyed Debbie. She quickly rushed up to get a good glimpse at the map.

Ten minutes later, Tippy returned and reported, "There's a huge, old tree, not too far from here, where we can set up a base camp inside the tree."

Tippy glanced at the map and commented, "The tree should be right where the road curves, sharply to the right. The Castle is a half mile beyond the curve. We move out in five minutes."

Beneath the giant tree, with branches that resembled a gnarled mess, Tippy pointed up into it and stated, "Our base will be up there."

"Ah, are you sure the tree isn't going to attack us? Asked Debbie. "This tree is a nightmare; it has to be at least ten feet in diameter at the base."

"Moe, you and Debbie cut down the small trees to form the floor and the walls. I'll scrounge around for the vines to tie things together. Don't forget, vaporize the tree stumps after you've cut the tree down," stated Tippy.

"Duh," replied Moe, "What do you think we are, morons?"

"No, I'm making sure; we have all our bases covered," answered Tippy.

By the time the sun had arched across the sky and was quickly setting, Debbie was putting the last of the grass on the roof.

"Time for the evening meal," bellowed Moe as she tossed Debbie an energy bar.

"Oh, joy! More cardboard," grumbled Debbie.

"At least we're not starving to death," remarked Moe.

"Before the Lord Jesus takes me home to be with Him, I will find a way to add flavor to these tasteless things they call energy bars."

Tippy stuck her head out of the tree hut and inquired, "You two going to stay out all night? Come on in."

"Why didn't you tell me you had a food basket of goodies?" questioned Moe. She then noticed a pile of clothes lying in a corner and stated, with a sneaky smile etched on her face, "You scarfed these, didn't you?"

"Well, not exactly. I posed as a beggar in desperate need, and before I knew it, I was loaded with more things than I needed, which tells me that the people in this dimension are nice. It's that Victoria woman who is evil. Now, chow down."

Indulging herself in a piece of meat, Moe hiked up to the garments, picked one up, and noticed a note attached to it that reads, I know who you are, where you came from. Please, help deliver us from the vicious queen who has kept us in bondage these past ten years."

"If the locals know we're here, then you can bet on it; the queen does, too," stated Moe.

"That's why we have to be extremely careful tomorrow," said Tippy. We should wear our Omega uniforms underneath the clothes I picked up today."

"Do we walk through the castle gate like everyone else?" inquired Moe. "If we do, we'll be caught, for sure."

How about if we hitch a ride underneath a passing wagon?" suggested Debbie.

Sounds like a plan," stated Tippy. "It's time we turned in for the night because tomorrow will be one long day."

Tippy shook her companions long before dawn and stated, "It's time. Choose what you'll wear from the clothing I picked up and put it on."

Moe groaned as she slipped into a light blue gown and inquired, "We have to get up before the sun? Not fair. Besides, my cloak sticks below my dress. Have you any suggestions?"

"Yeah," answered Tippy. Take hold of the bottom edge, fold it under the cape, and fasten it. Then, try to hide your mask and hat."

Hitching a ride under a wagon passing by the omega team made it safely into the Castle. Tippy whispered, "You two, check out the marketplace while I check out the Castle. If you get into trouble, call me."

4

Alex, the Tyrant

It was easy for Moe and Debbie to blend into the busy marketplace. A jolly, fat man eyed Moe's cane and said, "Nice cane you have there. Care to part with it? I'll give you a good deal on a goat."

Debbie smiled and moved silently on. Suddenly, a woman's screams for help resounded through the marketplace. But no one paid any attention to her desperate cries. Moe quickened her pace as she said, "Come on, Deb. There's trouble afoot."

Entering the main castle court, the two women gasped in horror as a woman with a burlap sack barely covering her nude body was chained to a tall stone column and was being brutally whipped. Moe muttered to Debbie, "I wonder what that poor thing did to warrant that kind of cruel punishment."

Debbie's eyes quickly danced around the courtyard in search of a reason to help the chained prisoner. Spotting a well off to one side, Debbie casually strolled to it, helped herself to a cup of water, and then asked sweetly, "Kind Sir, would it be alright if I gave that woman a cup of water?"

The palace guard gruffly answered, "No! It's forbidden!"

"What can a cup of water do? But refresh her parched lips."

"Okay, but hurry up about it!"

Debbie placed the cup on the ground while she helped the woman to her feet and shrieked in horror at the woman's grotesque features. The woman pleaded, "Debbie, it's me, Trudy, of Mystery's Three investigation Team. Please, help me."

After giving Trudy the water, Debbie slipped on her mask, ripped off her outer garment, showed her Omega Squad uniform, and shouted, "Try picking on someone your own size for a change!"

A crack from a whip sent Debbie's pistol flying. The next one caught Debbie's face. She screamed as she fell to the ground. The guard drew back his whip to beat her again. When the guard's eyes bulged, arched his back, then tumbled to the ground with a spear in it.

Moe hollered, "Now, it's personal!"

Debbie touched her wrist and said to Tippy, "We need help in the main courtyard, pronto!" Debbie then screamed, "Moe, Watch out! To your left!"

Moe yanked the spear out of the man and twisted around, catching another guard in the stomach. Then, two dozen men rushed into the courtyard, brandishing broad swords. Now surrounded, Moe inquired, "Do you have any suggestions, Deb?"

"Yeah, weapons on full, camouflage fields on and fire. They can't hit what they can't see."

Tippy jumped out of a second-story window and let out a shriek, sounding more animal than human, terrifying the guards. Tippy swooped down, grabbed Trudy, and flew off while Moe and Debbie casually strolled away, unseen.

Passing under a stone archway, Moe glanced up and commented, "Those little blue lights; they weren't there when we came in. Were they?"

Passing under the arch, their camouflage cloaks began to flicker. "Oh, crap! We've been made," as twelve castle guards surrounded them, one guard shouted, "We've got them, Sir!."

Alex, clad in a pale yellow robe trimmed in royal blue, strutted between the guards. Muttering, "Stupid lowlifes. Don't you know, you can't win." He chuckled, saying, "Let's make an example of them. Kill them and hang their dead bodies where everyone can see, as a warning to anyone who dares challenge Victoria, the queen."

Moe hollered, "Alex my sweet, Snap out of it! You're a child of the most high God! You can't do this!"

Alex shook his head as he staggered sideways close to Moe. She quickly reached around her back, grabbed her dagger, and placed it under Alex's throat, saying, "Drop your weapons, or I'll cut him a new smile."

Alex shouted, "Do it!"

Reluctantly, the guards dropped their swords and placed their hands over their heads. Debbie promptly fired her energy pistol, stunning them. Alex, noticing a slack in Moe's attention, bit her hand and then disappeared into a building before Moe could stun him.

As she nervously glanced around, Debbie suggested, "I think we need to beat a hasty retreat before reinforcements show up."

Back at the tree hut, Tippy was putting a dressing of leaves on Trudy's wounds.

With her head cocked to one side, Moe inquired, "You want to enlighten me on why you are putting leaves on Trudy's injuries instead of normal bandages?"

"This type of leaf will ease the pain and promote healing. When she is in stable condition, I'll bring her back through the rift and contact Sam. By the way, did any of you find Alex?"

"Yeah, he gave the order to have us killed. If I ever get my hands on that imp, I'll wring his neck," growled Moe.

"Easy there, girl. Remember who you are," commented Debbie. "He's under Victoria's control. What we need is a pheromone blocker. If one does exist."

Trudy moaned, "Thank you for saving my life."

Tippy questioned, "Trudy. What are you doing here?"

"The Mystery Three Team was investigating an odd swirling mass of air by the Black Pond. I made the mistake of touching it. The next thing I knew, I was here in this realm. After checking out the place for an hour, I tried to return, but the vortex was gone. Victoria thought I was a spy and locked me up. The next thing I know, I'm being shackled to a post in the courtyard, wearing nothing but a burlap bag. If I get my hands on that Alex, he'll wish he were never born because of what he did to me while I was locked up."

"Trudy. Do you think you can travel? I want to take you home."

Weeping, Trudy pleaded, "Please, don't! Look what they've done to my face! I'm a monster!"

Tippy reassured, "My people will be able to reconstruct your face. All they need is a picture."

"Do you think so?" questioned Trudy as a glimmer of hope began to grow.

"I know so. Now, let's get going. If you like, you can wear the clothes I gave me yesterday."

After dressing, Trudy placed a veil over her face and inquired, "Can you please take me directly to your people? I'm ashamed to have anyone see my hideousness."

"No problem, however, to keep your friends in the dark about you would not be fair."

"Well, okay, But just the Mystery's Three Team, that's all," demanded Trudy.

"When I return, we'll go after Alex," stated Tippy.

"Don't forget to bring back a thermos full of coffee. Better yet, make that two thermoses."

Moe leveled her gaze at Debbie and said, "I'm going to go and read the Word. That bout with the castle guards today was a little unsettling."

Later that evening, a relaxed Moe remarked, "You know, right about now, I could devour two meatball foot longs. The fruit was good, but I'm a meat eater."

"Sort of a short T-Rex," added Debbie.

"Cute. Not to change the subject, but what will we do about Alex? He has to be stopped."

"I know," Debbie said. "If he can't be persuaded to come back, he'll have to be taken out."

Moe hung her head and agreed. "Oh, by the way, do we have any more goodies left?"

"No, just cardboard tasting, energy bars."

"Then, toss me one, Deb, will you please? I might as well have something. My stomach is about to sue my backbone for lack of support. Or is it that my backbone is about to sue my stomach for lack of support? My brain has gone numb from lack of food, and I can't remember."

The next morning, Debbie's shoulder brushed against a cold stone wall. Wide-eyed, she sprang to her feet and said slowly, "Moe. We have a problem."

"Don't bug me. I want to get more Z-time."

Debbie bellowed, "Moe!"

Moe quickly opened her eyes, nervously felt the stone wall, and questioned, "How did we get in here? She then jumped to her feet, shouting as she glanced around the dungeon, "Door without room, Door without room! We're trapped! How are we going to get out!"

"Debbie chuckled and said, "Calm down, Moe. Stay with me, and don't you mean a room without doors?"

"Yeah, that too," answered Moe. "But how did they find us? That's what I'd like to know!"

"You snore loud enough to wake the dead."

"I do not," snapped Moe.

Debbie reached in back of her and grumbled, "Oh, man! They took my dagger and energy pistol." She smiled and said, "I still have my cane. Shall I blast a hole in the wall and make our escape?"

"Nah, let's hang around and find out what's happening."

Five minutes later, one of the walls began to vibrate and slowly slipped up into the ceiling. Alex merrily strolled in, followed by two castle guards, brandishing Moe's dagger, commenting, "Handy little weapon—lightweight, well balanced. You, ah, still plan to slit my throat? The way you rescued that lowlife was fantastic. The queen could use people like you."

"Forget it," bellowed Debbie.

"Don't be so hasty. All you have to do is plant a few small devices around your side of the opening to help the queen. No biggy."

"In a pig's eye, we will," shouted Moe.

Suddenly, the Lord flooded Moe with His peace, softening her countenance as she spoke, "Jesus loves you. Fight the wicked queen's influence over you Alex."

Alex's cocky, self-righteous attitude morphed into a forlorn expression as he whispered, "Moe. What are you doing here?"

Seizing Alex's moment of weakness, Moe grabbed the dagger from Alex's hand and flipped him onto the floor. She then threw her knife, hitting one guard in the stomach. Debbie drop-kicked the other guard, sending him stumbling backward and triggering the wall controls to trap Alex in the dungeon with the two women.

"Now, look what you've done, you lowlifes! Guards, guards, get me out of here!"

Debbie rested her arm on Alex's shoulder and questioned, "Lowlifes?"

"Get your hand off me," said Alex, shoving her aside.

Debbie jumped to her feet and belted Alex in the stomach, knocking the wind out of him. He leaned against a wall and moaned, "Sorry, I'm having difficulty fighting against the queen's control over me."

"Alex. Which wall is an outside wall?" questioned Moe

"That one," pointing to a wall behind her.

"It's time to leave this dump," stated Moe.

Moe spun around, placed her cane on her left arm, and fired. A wave of pale yellow energy shot out of the cane, incinerating the wall.

Alex crawled out of the dungeon after the women when a voice hollered, "Behind you!"

Alex crumpled to the ground as an arrow pierced his shoulder. Debbie immediately struck a fighting pose as a man in his late forties rushed up to them with his hands up, saying, "I'm on your side. I was trying to warn you that the queen's henchman was behind you."

"Thanks, but we need him," answered Moe.

"But he belongs to the queen," shouted the man.

"Makes no difference; he has to come with us."

"Okay," the man reluctantly replied, "follow me." The man grabbed the arrow sticking out of Alex and yanked it out; after putting it back in his quiver, he carried Alex to a small hut.

Ten minutes later, the man laid Alex on a cot. Tippy stepped out from the shadows and joyfully greeted her companions, saying, "I see you've captured Alex. By the way, this man gave us the food earlier." She questioned the man, "Do you think you can help him? He's from our dimension."

The man sighed and said, "You can call me Nimble. Because you ask, I'll see what I can do, but there's no guarantee it'll work." Nimble took a bottle and rubbed a small, sticky, pungent substance under Alex's nose. Then he said, "Your friend should be able to travel by tomorrow morning."

"I hope you don't mind me asking, but why is all the modern technology only in the castle?" Debbie questioned.

Nimble glared at her for a minute, then said sarcastically, "I think you already know the answer."

The next day, a tall, gaunt woman stepped out of a side room and stated, "Once he's back on your side of the opening, get him as far as you can from the rift. That will weaken Victoria's influence on him."

"Will do," replied Moe.

Later that day, by the dimensional rift in the field, Alex's demeanor slowly changed as Victoria's influence took over. Tippy muttered, "Not again." She grabbed Alex around his waist and dove through the opening, followed by Moe and Debbie. After securing Alex, Tippy contacted Sam, saying, "Alpha One, this is The Omega Strike Force. We need backup right away. Sam stepped through a portal a minute later, saying, "How are things?"

"Fine," we need to get Alex as far from this sight as possible, then set a watch over him to ensure he doesn't try to go through the rift again. After that's done, we need to devise a plan to eradicate Victoria before she destroys both dimensions."

Sam embraced Debbie and said, "I think you ladies need to take a rest before going back."

5

Decoy

Back at the Omega Base, Moe stored her MCW, changed into her street clothes, and then went to the kitchen and fixed herself a foot-long steak and cheese sandwich. Debbie headed for the hot tub to soothe her sore, aching muscles. Tippy found a quiet spot and studded the word. Two days later, she approached Moe as she was enjoying a tossed salad and inquired, "Are you going to visit Alex? In Willow City?"

"No, for one, he tried to have us killed, and I can't get that sinister laugh of his out of my mind while he was under the control of that queen. Is that Alex or a clever decoy?"

"Didn't you two have something going?" questioned Debbie.

"No, he gave me a place to crash until I could get back on my feet, and we fooled around on my bed once, but that's all!" answered Moe cryptically.

"Tippy suggested that we pay Alex a visit to find out what he knows about Victoria and the castle's layout so we can plan an all-out assault."

"Right now, I couldn't care less about Alex, Victoria, and the battle. Leave me alone!" growled Moe.

"What's eating you? I thought you might like company, seeing you've been by yourself these past few days."

"I'm fine. Now, go away!"

"Okay, Moe. What's bugging you?"

30

"It's me! I'm bugging me," shouted Moe, "I didn't like some of the things I had to do while we were in the land of Tob. I'm having a difficult time getting over the fact that I killed someone." Moe screamed as tears streamed down her face, "I can still see his face when my dagger stuck into his stomach. Now, leave me alone!"

Debbie's voice softened as she queried, "Have you brought it before the Lord?"

"No, I assumed I had to deal with it myself."

Debbie remained silent while seeking the Lord Jesus for His wisdom about Moe. She then stated, "If you had a son who isolated himself from you every time he had a problem, how would you feel?"

Moe smiled and said, "Point taken; thanks, I guess I have to pray before I read the Word from now on."

"Talk to you later," I'm going to fire up the Alpha Wing; Tippy wants to leave for Willow City within the hour."

Later, as Debbie prepared the Alpha Wing for takeoff, Moe stared out the window, struggling with her inadequacy. Suddenly, an overwhelming peace flooded her being, driving out the fear. Then, the Lord spoke to her gently, "Peace, be still, be not afraid. For I am with you." In His presence, Moe became aware of her sins of fear, doubt, and unbelief, and she immediately asked, "Lord, please forgive me." The soothing forgiveness rushed over her soul, cleansing her. With renewed confidence in her ability, Moe drifted off to sleep.

Ten minutes before Willow City, Moe questioned, "Guys, we have a slight problem. These Omega outfits are great; however, we need names to go with them. I can't walk up to Debbie, who is clad in her cape and hat, and say, "Hey Deb, give me a hand. It would defeat the purpose of having a mask."

"Good thinking," answered Debbie, "I like the name, "Night Walker.""

"Ahhh, I was thinking of Beta, Gamma, and Delta as names," stated Tippy, "Deb, you be Delta, I'll be Gamma, and Moe, you be Beta."

Debbie pipped up and queried, "Shall we name Sam Alpha One? Seeing, he's the top dog."

"Everyone agrees?" questioned Tippy.

"Okay, everyone, take your seats; we are about to land," stated Debbie.

Tippy slipped in the co-pilot's seat and suggested, "There's a field south of the city where you can set her down. Willow City has no landing field. But you can count on Prince Blue to greet us with the military."

Coming out of Alpha Wing, clad in Omega Strike Force uniforms, they greeted Prince Blue of the Will-of-the-Wisps. Gamma stated sternly, "We've come here to question Alex."

Blue stared into Gamma's eyes, then smiled and said, "Sure, no problem, I'll be glad to assist the Omega Strike Force. I'll post a guard by your ship. Tara, my gal Friday, will show you the way."

Will-of-the-wisp Tara inquired, "Would you like to rest up first?"

"No, thank you," answered Beta.

The Omega Strike Force was approaching the house, and Alex darted out the back door to escape. Tara took flight and snatched him up, setting him down in front of the Strike Force.

Alex began to holler, "I'm innocent! I didn't do It!"

"If you're innocent, then you have nothing to worry about," stated Gamma. "Now, what can you tell us about the queen's castle? How many men does she have?"

"Well, let's see, there's the wall, the courtyard, and the castle, with a nice throne room. Is there anything else I can help you with?"

"Can the sarcasm, Alex? You know what we want. Where is the mechanism that controls the rift? How do we shut it down? Is there another way inside the castle walls besides the main gate?" questioned Beta.

"If you will excuse me, I have a nasty headache." Alex turned to leave when Beta grabbed his arm, saying, "You are going nowhere, mister, until we're finished with you. Now, Where is the vortex machine?"

Avoiding the question, Alex answered, "My memory is foggy concerning the queen. How can I tell you about something I don't remember? So, back off!"

Gamma picked up Alex by his collar and growled, "Do you want to be the first human tent stake? If you don't answer and tell us what we need to know, so help me, I'll pound you in the ground! Right here!"

"Alex smirked, then said, "Remember, as long as I'm in Willow City, I'm protected by their laws, which say you can't force me to confess. So go ahead. You'll be the one doing time, not me."

Gamma let go of Alex, knowing he was right. Beta smiled and asked sweetly, "Alex, how much have you read the Bible since you've been here?"

"Never read the book."

"How's Jim and Ella's Bible study going? Have they gotten in any heavy discourses lately?"

"I've never been there. Like I said before. I have a headache. If you don't have any serious charges against me, leave before I file a complaint of harassment against the three of you."

When Alex spun around to leave, Beta spotted a red pendant around Alex's neck and asked, "You care to explain the jewelry?"

"It's something I picked up around here," answered Alex. "No biggy"

"Let me see that," asked Tara. "When coming here from another planet, anything of value must be declared. I'll have to seize that to determine its worth."

With lightning-fast reflexes, Will-o-the-wisp, Tara yanked the pendant off Alex.

He screamed, "You idiot! Then, he morphed into one of Victoria's guards. Tara handed it to Gamma and said, "Here, you might need this."

The guard laughed, then said sarcastically, "Oh, I'm sorry; you'll have to cancel your assault on the castle. The queen closed the opening. We'll still have access to your dimension somewhere else. But you won't find it."

Tara summoned the Wisp police and said, "He is dangerous. Search every inch of him. Then, lock him up."

Back at the Alpha Wing, Delta contacted Sam and reported, "Alpha One, This is Alpha Wing reporting in. We interrogated Alex and discovered that he was an imposter. For now, the Wisps have him locked up in a secure place. However, we need confirmation that the queen has closed the rift."

"This is Alpha One. Good job, come on home; you deserve a rest. Alpha One out."

In their street clothes, Moe, Tippy, and Debbie stepped through the portal into Thor's office. Tippy questioned as she glanced around, "I wonder where everyone is?" Suddenly, a five-foot, five-inch tall woman in her mid-twenties barged into the dimly lit office and shouted, "Hold it right there! No one makes a move, or I'll use it!"

Tippy leveled her gaze at the woman and inquired, "Cathy, you're going to beat us with a sandwich? Where is everyone?"

"It's three o'clock in the morning," answered Cathy, "I was in the cafeteria rummaging for food when I heard a noise coming from Thor's office."

"Oh, This is Moe; she'll stay with us for a few days. Can she bunk with you?"

"Sure. Hey Moe, what'd know?" inquired Cathy as she turned to leave the office with Moe.

Moe groaned as she shook her head.

"Moe, what's purple, has five eyes and orange legs?" questioned Cathy

"I don't know. What?"

"I don't know either, but it's crawling up your leg."

Moe glanced up, pleaded, "Lord, help." and swatted it.

MiFFd-morning the following beautiful day, Moe found a shady palm tree on Crater Lake beach and sat down, scribbling in the sand with a stick, feeling left out. Ten minutes later, Cathy merrily strolled up to her and asked, "Do you mind If I join you?"

"Only if you promise not to tell any more of those bad jokes."

"Deal," Cathy quickly sat down and remarked, "You look like you haven't a friend in the world. What's on your mind?"

"Me, coming here was a mistake."

How so?" questioned Cathy.

"Seeing Debbie and Tippy, with their families, brought back the pain of my parents dumping me when I was sixteen."

"I'm sorry to hear that. Do you know where they are?"

"Moe just shook her head, no."

"Hey, I'm doing a few comic skits; you wanna help?"

"Well, I don't know."

"Come on. It'll be a blast. What do you have to lose besides your pride?"

"Okay. What do I do?" questioned Moe.

Just after the noon meal, Thor approached Moe and said, "There's a meeting on the fifth floor in ten minutes. Be there. Oh, Moe, you still have some pie behind your left ear."

On the fifth floor, Thor touched a keypad and stated, "Computer, run the Particle Acceleration program, 'Vortex.'

"Loaded. Enter when ready," answered the computer.

The door opened into a large room with a three-dimensional map of the queen's castle and surrounding area. Thor announced to everyone, "Before the rift closed, we received data from the probe that we had launched earlier. Sam, you want to take it from here?"

Sam pointed to the castle and said, "The place has fifteen-foot thick walls, with a dry moat. There are four low-yearling energy cannons mounted on the castle walls. The queen has only five hundred men guarding it. Piece of cake, right?"

Everybody eagerly agreed. "Wrong! Shouted Sam, "The castle is situated in a narrow pass, which should make it an easy target. However, there are two lightning cannons on each mountain, housing a thousand men each and protecting the castle. The cannons must be taken out before Blue sends his troops in; if we're not fast enough, the castle guards will activate their second line of defense.

As you can see, the castle has a high mound, concealing a tunnel that circles the outer perimeter. Once in there, it will be impossible to get them out. So, the element of surprise is of the utmost importance. One slip-up could spell disaster. Any questions?"

One security guard stood up and said, "Sir, couldn't we open a portal and flood the dry moat?"

"Good Idea," answered Sam, But the portals won't work there."

Another guard suggested, "Sir, what if we mind the doorways leading into the tunnels and prevent them from using them?"

"I like it. How soon can you get your men together?"

"Already done."

"Good, report here in thirty minutes and access the simulation 'Vortex Castle.'

Tippy questioned, "Sam. Have they found where the new vortex is located?"

"No, But we've got every possible man and Will-o-the-wisp available, on the lookout. Just then, charcoal gray clouds gathered in the room as Blue strolled out, saying, "The guard talked, but he never told us where the next vortex was going to be. Sorry."

"Ah, Blue, how did you manage to get him to spill his guts?"

Blue grinned and said, "After almost being eaten by a fierce monster, he told us everything."

"Isn't that violating your laws? Forcing a confession out of him?" questioned Sam.

"Pretty much. But now, we have to figure out what to do with a basket case for a castle guard. My men are ready; give the word."

The new vortex was found and in no time the castle was taken unfortunately Alex and the queen escaped.

6

The visitor

Detective Darrin, a six-foot-tall man with brown hair and hazel eyes who lives in Spokane, Washington, answered his iPhone, saying, "Can I help you Sir,"

"I'm Alex Smashburger and I'm looking for two women, one is shoer and the other is about six feet tall. I'll send my man Albert to your office with a photo with a complete description of them."

Just a moment, there is someone at the door." Darrin opened the door, looked down at the vast brown box on his stoop, muttered, "What in the world is in that?" and dragged it into his western style living room. Upon opening it, Darrin stared at a dissembled female manakin muttering, "I wonder who at the station sent me this? I know Pete is always trying to hook me up with a blind date, so it was probably him trying to be funny."

Once he had assembled the Manakin, he stared at the tall, nude, willowy woman with light brown hair. Slowly, lid his hand over her soft body and patted her bare butt, saying, "Why would Pete send me a female manakin that has everything a normal woman has? I better put this monstrosity in my walk-in closet before someone comes to the door and thinks I'm fooling around with a naked store manakin,"

The next morning, Darrin had a bowl of cornflakes and rushed off to work.

Later, he sat at his desk talking to a young man in his twenties, saying, "So you are Albert and this is the women I you to be on the lookout for."

Darrin stared at the photo and said, "Strange this is a picture of the storm mannequin that came to my door yesterday."

"Be careful store mannequin as you call it is a new invention called a Mandroid. I'll be by within a day or two to take her off your hands. Oh and here's $100,000 for your troubles."

At home, Darrin opened the walk-in closet in his bedroom to get out his clothes for the next day. She stared at the mannequin, thinking, "I must be losing it because I never dressed her in my good blue shirt and pants," and had taken off the shirt when the mannequin spoke up, saying, "What do you think you are doing? Leave my clothes alone, you pervert, and the next time you grab my bare butt, I will slap you silly."

A shocked Darrin stared at the mannequin and said, "Wait a minute. You're a dummy made out of. I don't know what, and you're not supposed to be talking."

My name is Ruthie, and I'm not some stupid store mannequin. I'm a Mandroid that was put together by a dimwit Alex, and now he's trying to kill me. So, leave my clothes alone before I pound the crap out of you."

"Big talk coming from something that's supposed to be standing in a store window."

Ruthie grabbed the shirt out of Darrin's hand, put it on then walked out of the walk-in closet and into the kitchen, with Darrin following her. She grabbed a glass of green iced tea from the fridge, saying, "If I am gonna be staying here, you need to get some decent food in this house."

Darrin stated, "Wait a minute, Manakin, let's get one thing straight. This is my home, and what I say goes."

Ruthie glanced around and said, "With that attitude, no wonder you're still single. Now, how about fixing me some breakfast before I perish from starvation,"

"For a manikin, you sure are demanding. The cereal is in the top left cupboard, the bowls are in the upper right cupboard, and the spoons are in the drawer to your right, so knock yourself out."

After Ruthie had her cereal and banana, she asked, "Where am I gonna sleep?"

Darrin brought Ruthie to the garage apartment on the left side of the house, saying, "You stay here, and you will provide your own food and clothes,"

Ruthie grabbed Darrin by his shirt, saying, "Hey, Smart Boy, you found me, so I am your responsibility, like it or not," She spotted a white van swiftly approaching with the side door open, shouted, "Hit the dirt!" and tackled Darem as a spray of bullets riddled the garage door.

Darrin smiled up at Ruthie on top of him, put his hands on her back, saying, "Thanks for saving my life." And kissed her lips.

Ruthie removed his hands from the lower part of her back, saying, "Get that thought out of your mind because it is not gonna happen," she stood and hauled Darrin to his feet, saying, "We need to set some ground rules. When I am in your house, you will be dressed, and I don't wash your back when you are in the shower,"

In Ruthie's garage apartment, she thought, *"I need some clothes, especially a booby catcher."* Ruthie thought momentarily, then stated, "If I gotta, I gotta." Entered Darrin's home and said, "You, my dear man, need a good body rub to get those lazy muscles of yours back in shape."

Darrin smiled and said, "Sounds good to me. Where do you want me to be?"

"Lay on your bed with just a towel covering your bottom; then I'll come in and stimulate those muscles. Oh, I forgot to tell you I charge $300 for my services. In advance."

Ruthie's hands glided smoothly down Darrin's back, with each movement flowing seamlessly into the next. She listens intently to the quiet sighs escaping his lips, relishing the knowledge that she's bringing her relief and pleasure. Ruthie's touch became even more sensitive, tracing the muscles of his body with the utmost care and dedication.

Darrin stated, "That feels so good. Don't even think about stopping,"

"Absolutely," stated Ruthie with renewed energy, delicately working her way down his spine, applying just the right amount of pressure. Each stroke left Darrin visibly relaxed as the knots melted away, leaving him feeling rejuvenated and restored.

Darrin lying face down on the bed with a bath towel across his bottom and asked, "Can I get dressed now?"

"Why don't you lie there and relax and my advice is that you have a good rub-down at least once a week, so I'll schedule your next rub-down for 10:00 AM every Saturday. This is just FYI: If you find me shut off for any reason, I still have the capacity to know what's going on and what part of my body is being touched."

A slightly embarrassed Darrin stated, "I was just trying to put you together and didn't mean to rub your butt. By the way, exactly what is a Mandroid?"

"I'll take that weak excuse as an apology. But if you ever do that to me again, I'll slap you silly. A Mandroid has all artificial organs in its body. The heart pumps real blood through the veins; the lungs pump real oxygen to keep a human brain in the skull alive. The arms and legs are robotic; however, I have emotions and can feel pain, heat, and cold. I can also snuggle with a man, and no, we are not going to try it. Now, if you will excuse me, I'm going to the store to buy myself some clothes so I can look like a woman again,"

A short time later, in Lolo Boutique, Ruthie had spent all she had and was walking out of the store when she almost tripped on a thirty-five-inch tall girl. She apologized and then asked, "Can I help you with anything? Is there any place you need to go? Because one of my neighbors was kind enough to drive me here, maybe she'll take you where you need to go,"

The girl stated my name is Tina, and I'm 29. I need a place to stay for a few days. Do you think you could put me up until I get my act together?"

Ruthie studied Tina's ears and questioned, "Why are your ears pointed,"

Tina nervously glanced around and then stated, "It's a congenital disability,"

Ruthie put Tina on her right shoulder, saying, "I don't want you to get trampled on, so you can sit up here until we get to the car,"

In Ruthie's garage home, Tina sat on a stool at the eating counter took a bite of her Peanut butter and jelly sandwich, and then said, "Thank you for putting me up for a few days."

"No problem. Now tell me who you really are and no more birth defects stories."

"I am a Sprite on the run from Alex, who wants to put me in a cage and then give me to Queen Victoria as a pet." She then turned off the energy field, hiding her transparent wing.

Ruthie stated, "I went to Alex's lab for a simple operation and woke up in this idiotic mechanical contrivance. In other words, I'm a Mandroid on the run from the dumb Alex who put me in this thing."

"You're a Mandroid!" shouted Tina. Far out! How did you escape?"

"I had a nurse show me around the huge lab, and when we came across a large box, I had her shut me off and pack me in it. That's how I wound up here. Oh, by the way, watch out for Darrin, who lives in the house attached to the garage and is frisky."

A short time later, Tina was sleeping on the couch when Darrin walked in and gave Ruthie a long hug, passionately kissing her. But was interrupted by a call on his cell phone. After he ended the call Darrin stated, "That call was from a gentleman looking for you."

Ruthie fixed herself then stated firmly, "This garage apartment is my home and it doesn't mean you can barge in my home and take advantage of me. Also you do not walk into my home unannounced because I may be in my skivvies. Because if you do, I will defend myself, and trust me, you do not want that to happen."

"Enough with the chitchat. I need to hide you and your little friend before he gets here."

Darrin led Ruthie and Tina into the walk-in closet, then pulled down a wall, turning the walk-in closet into a regular closet, hiding Tina and Ruthie behind it. Some 10 minutes later, Darrin answered the doorbell and greeted a well-dressed man in his mid-thirties. The man introduced himself as Alex, showed Darrin a picture of Ruthie, and then stated in a heavy German accent, "I've come to understand that you have this woman."

"I have no idea what you are talking about. But if you like to search my home, you're welcome, but I have to warn you you're not going to find her."

Alex diligently searched Darrin's home for almost 2 hours and didn't find Ruthie, then stormed out the door.

Some three hours had passed, and Ruthie and Tina began to wonder if Darrin had forgotten them. Suddenly, the closet opened, and a rugged-looking man in his fifties clad in a red shirt and blue pants, six feet tall, with dark brown curly hair and a VanDyke, stood in front of them.

Tina quickly flew behind Ruthie as she cried, "Please don't hurt us."

The man never said a word but escorted them into the living room. He turned to Darrin and asked, "What are you doing with a Sprite and a Mandroid in your home?"

Darrin looked at Ruthie and Tina, then stated, "You two can relax because he's not going to harm you. This is Sam, *Alpha One*, and his upcoming protege Tippy. It seems Alex is from the other side of the Galaxy, and I have difficulty believing anything they've told me. Anyway, they look harmless." Darrin stated, "Sam, you can ask them all the questions you want. I promise you they will cooperate."

A six-foot-tall young woman with short brown hair looked at Tina on her right side and asked, "What's a cute little thing like you doing on Earth? Besides trying to get yourself killed?"

Tina, sitting in Tippy's right hand, showed a weak smile and then stated, "I'm a Fairy Sprite from a planet on the outer reaches of the Galaxy. I wasn't watching where I was flying, entered some strange pink fog and wound up on this planet, fighting for my life. That's when I met Ruthie."

An angry Ruthie stated, "I am from Losier settlement a few miles north of Tricadia-Shelia, New Brunswick, Canada. Doctor Alex told me that I had a severe illness and needed surgery right away, and the only place I could get it was in Spokane, Washington, and he would pay all my expenses. When I woke up from my surgery, I was shocked when I discovered that I was in somebody else's body. That's when the nurse told me Alex had put my brain in this stupid mechanical contraption called a Mandroid. All I want is to get out of this mechanical contrivance and have my own body back."

"You've have my full cooperation."

Tippy opened a 10-foot pale blue portal shaped like the Greek letter omega, saying, "Right this way,"

7

A new world

Ruthie exited the portal, stood on a round platform, and asked, "Where am I? Was I given some sleeping medication to make me believe I'm on the other side of the Galaxy? They'll have to get up pretty early in the morning to pull the wool over my eyes. Now, where am I,"

Ruthie stared at Tippy's transparent wings on her back and said, "Nice, but I think it's a little bit too much on the fantasy side to be real."

Tippy took Ruthie outside and stated, "Look up and tell me what you see?"

Ruthie's eyes widened as she whispered, "I am now totally weirded out. I see what looks like an asteroid belt mixed in with stars and a planet." Ruthie then gazed at Tippy, saying, "I suppose your wings are real,"

Tippy smiled, saying, "They sure are see for yourself."

Ruthie touched Tippy's wings, grew silent, then stated, "Oh my gosh," and passed out.

Sprite Tina was sitting on the nightstand beside Ruthie's bed in the Infirmary. When she opened her eyes, she said, "Welcome to Omega Base, on the planet Dicapl on the other side of the Galaxy. Don't worry, you'll get used to being here and seeing all kinds of strange stars and sites. Oh, by the way, Sam's wife, Dora, will explain the Omega One Headquarters to you. Then Sam wants to question you about what you did to enrage Alex, who will be in in a few minutes. Talk to you later; I've got a date with a blanket on Crater Lake Beach."

A short time later, Tina found an out-of-the-way spot on the beach of Crater Lake. Spread her yellow and pink blanket on the sand. Took off her short-sleeved white top and blue slacks, then stretched out on the blanket in her skimpy bright yellow two-piece bathing suit.

A tall, dark figure stopped at the foot of Tina's blanket and stared at her. She stated with her eyes closed, "Whoever you are, could you please move to the left or the to the right because you're blocking my sun,"

The man threw his hand over Tina's mouth, muzzling her screams and dragged her into the jungle.

Tina's heightened senses suddenly kicked in, and she noticed that her abductor had rough hands and the type of aftershave he wore. She t heard a buzzing noise and knew they were passing by a bee's nest. She twisted her head so her mouth was free and shouted. "Ouch! Stupid bee stung my sit-down! Watch out, Mister, you may get stung! As soon as the man loosened his grip on Tina, she saw her chance to wiggle free and flew to a high branch, wiggled her butt at him saying, "You can't get me." Then she climbed to the top of the tree. Once Tina reached the very top, she was above the jungle canopy and flew back to the Omega One Headquarters.

Ruthie was walking out of the cafeteria, munching on a hotdog, saw Tina badly disheveled and questioned, "What in the world happened to you?"

"I was enjoying myself on the beach when some guy grabbed me and dragged me into the jungle. Fortunately, I was able to squirm loose. So whoever was after us on Earth is here on planet Dicapl, so be careful, Ruthie, that somebody doesn't drag you off somewhere. Oh, by the way, someone by the name of Patsy wants to talk to you."

Just then, Darrin walked by with a cup of coffee; Ruthie took hold of her left shoulder, pushed it in, and rotated the arm backward, took it off and belted Darrin across the head with it, saying, "What's the big idea taking off when we were in the middle of lunch,"

"Thanks a lot, Mannequin. You made me spill my coffee, and I left because I had something to do,"

Ruthie hit Darrin on the back of the head with her detached arm again, saying, "Hey numb-numb, I'm a Mandroid, not a mannequin that's spelled M-A-N-D-R-O-I-D,"

Tina caught a whiff of Darrin's aftershave, which made her think about the person who kidnapped her. But she was distracted when Tippy walked by. Tina flew up to her and asked, "Would it be alright with you if I have story time in the cafeteria this afternoon?"

"Sure, go ahead,"

The cafeteria was crowded with people as Sprite Tina stood on a high pedestal and shared one enchanting story after the other with a crowd of listeners who hung on every word. She then stated, "The last story this afternoon goes like this. The evening haze filled the garden, which bloomed only at midnight; its flowers were said to be made of Stars sparkling under the moon's embrace. A curious wanderer walked in every night seeking consolation among the flowers and found secrets carried by the wind, a tale of romance between moon and stars. The stranger left in the morning with a smile and joy in his heart. But returned that evening for more peace that the wind seemed to whisper. Then one evening, the flowers surrounded the stranger, and was carried away on a cloud of bliss, and was never seen again."

As people were walking out, Tina spotted a tall man in jeans and a blue flannel shirt and said, "Hey, Sentinel One, best bud, how has your day going? I haven't seen you in a long time."

"Tina, how about a hug? I know, keep the hug PG13?"

"I love being here at the Omega One Headquarters and being able to tell my stories."

"I remember the great little stories you used to tell."

"Maybe we could go on an adventure on this vegetation-covered planet and discover wonders that nobody knows about the way we used to,"

"Just name the day and time, and I'll be there because I'm a storyteller, too." Sentinel One gently touched Tina's side and tickled her," She hollered, "Eeeek! Hey, that's not fair. I'm super ticklish, but that's all right, we're friends. But watch out because I'm armed with a super tickle assault."

A week later, Tina approached Sentinel One, and he said, "*Alpha One* wants me to search for Alex because he knows where Queen Victoria opened the new vortex. Do you wanna join me?"

"Okay, and I'll call a tickle truth."

About an hour later, somewhere in the jungle north of the Omega One Headquarters, several energy blasts struck a nearby tree, sending Sprite Tina into a thorny bush then tumbled to the ground where a giant snake wrapped around her chest and stomach. Sentinel One swiftly killed the snake and asked, "Are you alright?"

"No, I am not. That bush I fell into cut me up pretty bad, and my wings hurt."

"Stay down,"

Several more energy blasts almost hit Sentinel One. He returned fire, picked up the wounded Sprite, and ducked into a nearby cave as the sky opened, dropping a deluge of rain. Sentinel One removed his backpack, built a cozy fire, and stared at an injured Tina. Spread his sleeping bag by the fire, then touched her wing muscles, causing Tina to cry out in pain. Sentinel One stated, "I am sorry to tell you, Little One, but you have a dislocated wing, along with multiple cuts and bruises all over you. I'm gonna have to take off your clothes and lay you on your stomach so I can bandage your body. Then I'm gonna have to put your wing back in place, and it's going to hurt big time,"

The gutsy Sprite stated, "I've never been naked in front of a man before. But Go ahead as long as you're gonna help me get better."

Sentinel One carefully removed Tina's clothes, tended to the multiple cuts on her tiny body, Tina then shrieked as waves of searing pain coursed through her tiny body, causing her to pass out when he snapped her wing back in place.

Because there was no way Sentinel One could dress Tina in the condition she was in. He crawled in the sleeping bag with his shirt off, lay on his side, and held a nude, shivering Sprite against his bare chest, praying the heat from his body would keep her from going into shock.

In the morning, Sentinel One inquired, "You alright, Tina?"

Tina enjoyed the warmth of Sentinel One's body and stated, "I'm hurting really bad from where I was hit in the shoulder by that energy blast and the thorn bush I fell into,"

A concerned Sentinel one questioned, "Would you like it if you snuggled with me until you feel better?"

"Oh, could I please,"

Sometime later, Tina became playful with Sentinel One, hinting to him that she wanted him.

Sentinel One asked, "Are you sure you want to fool around? Because I'm 6 feet and you're just a little bit of a thing."

"Yes I am sure because I want you more than you know. Less talk, more action."

When they were finished being intimate, Tina smiled and curled up on Sentinel One's bare chest.

Kayli Aubrette of Sprite Security, a feisty twenty-eight inch tall Sprite clad in a deep blue uniform shouted, "Hey, human, what are you doing to that Sprite? Or do I want to know?"

Tina sat up and covered herself, saying, "Sentinel One's my guardian and protector, and is helping me recover from a bad injury."

"That's not what I saw when I flew into the cave a short while ago."

Sentinel One dressed, stood, and asked, "What do you think Tina needs?"

Kayli examined Tina's injuries and then stated, "For a human, you did a pretty good job. Please leave the cave to give Tina some privacy so I can do a brief preliminary exam."

Once Tina had the proper bandage around her body and wing muscles, she dressed and had Sentinel One carry her back to the Omega One Headquarters. But she would not listen to Sentinel One about the opened vortex so they forgot about it.

About two days later, in the Omega One Headquarters' Infirmary, Tina approached Sentinel One and stated, "Looks like I'm grounded for a while. Would you mind carrying me to the beach?" Hoping to spend more time in Sentinel One's arms.

Ruthie rushed up to Tina, knelt, and said, "I heard you were injured. What happened?"

Tina smiled, saying, "I had one of those days where I should have stayed in bed. But things brightened up when I spent the night cuddled up to Sentinel One, and now we are as close as a Sprite could be to a human male. Which means we were intimate with each other all night. Hey, you wanna join Sentinel One and me on the beach?"

Ruthie glared at Sentinel One with contempt and stated, "You should be ashamed of yourself for doing such a thing to that poor little Sprite?"

Tina wrapped her arm around Sentinel One's left leg and shouted, "Just kidding, just kidding. I was injured really bad, so Sentinel One took care of my injuries and held me against his chest all night to keep me from going into shock. Now, shall we make our way down to the beach? Oh, by the way, where is Darrin?"

"You mean Meathead? Don't know, don't care,"

"Yeah, you do because you and Darrin make a great couple,"

Ruthie gagged and then stated, "Meathead is not my type, no way, no how."

Tina smiled and then stated, "I saw how you are starry-eyed when you are around Darrin,"

"You need glasses, Little One, because, to me, Darrin is barf city."

On the beach of Crater Lake, Sentinel One spread a green blanket on the white sand then put a blue cooler next to it. Tina removed her clothes revealing a skimpy two-piece, red paisley bathing suit and made herself comfortable on the blanket next to Sentinel One in his jean cutoffs. He studied Tina's body and questioned, "What happened to all your cuts and bruises? They're gone."

"Sprites are resilient, peppy little things that quickly bounce back from an injury. Now, can you put some suntan lotion on my little body before I look like a lobster?"

Ruthie sat on the blanked with Tina and Sentinel One in her beige slack suit and remained silent.

The sun hung low, painting the sky in a deep yellow, when a woman in a fancy dark tan two-piece bathing suit approached Ruthie and said. I'm Patsy, and you're the person I believe is the new Mandroid."

"Yeah, so what of it," snapped Ruthie.

"I'm here to help you understand how to maintain your new body and what to expect."

Ruthie growled, "You don't look like a Mandroid, but all I want to know is, where's that creep Akex who did this to me."

Patsy pointed to a small building on the left side of the bathhouse and said," In that building is a hot tub full of mineral oil that Mandroid should soak in at least once a week. By your attitude, I say it's about time you soaked for a long time."

"I do not want to soak in oil and be slimy for the rest of the day."

"Yeah, you do because the mineral oil will lubricate your joints, which will help you feel a lot better. Then I'll show you how to turn yourself off and back on when you want to."

"And how do you know all this?"

Patsy removed her left arm and said, "As you can see, I'm just like you. Now let's get those joints lubricated."

When Ruthie and Patsy were gone, Sentinel One stated, "Tina, please don't tell people what we did the night you were injured."

Tina stated, "When I came too, you were curled up against my back with me in your arms, and sexy ideas quickly flashed in my little head about the kinky things you did to me while I was passed out. Then, the fear that you forced yourself on me while I was unconscious and figured I was going to give birth to your baby in nine months. So without thinking, I spilled the beans, as you humans would say."

Sentinel One gently rubbed Tina's back, saying, "Fear can put all kinds of stupid thoughts in one's mind just to get a person worked up. All I did was massage your back, hoping to ease the pain when I put your wing back in place. After you passed out, I placed you on your side in my sleeping bag and curled up to you, hoping the heat from my body would keep you warm because you were shivering pretty bad. A couple of times through the night, I heard you moaning in your sleep, so I gently rubbed your bare back, which calmed you down."

Tina sat up and stated, "I'm a 35-inch twenty-nine-year-old Sprite who threw her modesty out the window so you could take care of my needs. Oh, and I enjoyed going all the way with you in the morning." Tina stood, hugged Sentinel One, and then stated, "We are close friends, bosom buddies through thick or thin. If you need help or someone to talk to, I'll be there by your side night or day. If you're lonely, we'll put on our comfy flannel PJs, curl up in a cozy blanket together by a crackling fire, and tell stories about days gone by."

8

Darrin's assault

A faint scream for help went unnoticed as Sprite Misty struggled desperately to stay afloat. Darrin tore out of the jungle, clad in jeans and no shirt, raced down the beach, dove in, and quickly swam to the Sprite that had just disappeared below the water.

Darrin carried the unconscious Misty to shore, lay her on the sand, and applied artificial respiration to the unconscious Sprite. When Darrin went to breathe air into Misty's lungs, she wrapped her arms around his neck and gave him a long kiss, thankful to be alive.

Once, Darrin had pried the Sprite's arms off his neck. He stood to walk away only to have the Sprite wrap her arms around his right leg, saying, "Aw, Don't go away, you hunk of a man; I've waited all my life for you."

Sentinel One approached Darrin and pried the Sprite off of him with her hollering, "Don't leave me, my love; I'll grow taller, I promise; please don't leave me, my love.

Moe, aka Beta, a woman five feet two inches tall with brown hair and eyes, approached Sprite Mysty, placed her hand on her back, and said, "Do you want to tell me why you are chasing a human?"

"The other day, I was in the Galaxy Diner enjoying my frozen treat when Darrin joined me. He told me how pretty I was and bought me a Big Juicy. Then, on the way to my home with Darrin, I had a big itchy between my wings. Then, when we were in my home, I lay on my couch, and

Darrin took care of my itchy, which felt so good. We then sat on the sofa, talking for hours about his job on Earth as a Detective. Darrin was about to say goodnight when Alex burst into the front door, knocked Darrin out, picked me up, and was on the way out the door with me hollering for help. That's when you ran across the front lawn, dropped and kicked Alex, which sent me tumbling through the air. Before you could react, Alex raced away into the night. I staggered to my feet, rushed back in, and tended to Darrin's head wound. He took me to a diner for the morning meal, which was very romantic. But it hurt when I saw him kissing Miss Vilma Puckett from the lab, and he has been ignoring me ever since."

Moe stated, "Maybe you misunderstood Darrin, and he was just being nice to you."

Misty stated firmly, "While we were making out on my couch, Darrin did what a Sprite would do when he wanted to commit to be her mate. I agreed and gave him my response. The romantic morning meal at the Galaxy diner sealed our relationship. Now he's seeing that cheap floozy Miss Puckett, which goes against sprites moral law concerning a couple's engagement."

"Are you sure about that?"

"Yes, I am sure. As part of Sprite Security, I was doing my normal fly over the jungle to check if there were any moral characters lurking around the jungle. That's when I spotted Darrin and Miss Pucket on the ground, wrapped in each other's arms. They were doing well, I won't say. Yes, I am sure, because why do you think Darrin had his shirt off and lipstick all over his face."

"So you took it upon yourself to distract Darrin and fake a drowning."

Misty lowered her head, saying, "Guilty as charged."

"Can you take me to where you spotted Darrin and Miss Pucket?"

"Sure can, just follow me,"

Several hundred feet in the jungle, Moe stared at an area of flattened vegetation. She placed her hands on the ground and said, "Yes, there were two people at this spot a short while ago because I can still feel the warmth from their bodies."

Misty touched her computer watch, saying, "Miss Pucket, meet me in the Arboretum in about 10 minutes because I have something very, very important to discuss with you."

In a spot of the garden where there were beautiful multiple-colored bushes, Miss Pocket was dressed in tan slacks, a white blouse, and a lab coat and slowly walked up to Misty and Tina. She greeted them and asked, "If you wanted to talk to me, why is this off-worlder here?"

"Moe is here to keep me in check for what I'm about to tell you. If you correctly remember, some years ago, you were more than romantically involved with a man who caused a lot of problems for the Omega One Headquarters. Sam didn't throw your Butt in jail for the rest of your life but gave you a job in the lab. Today, you were seen on the ground in the jungle naked, wrapped in Darrin's arms, doing things I'm ashamed to say. There's nothing wrong with romancing a bow, but what you two were doing wasn't right. Now, if my boss Moonbeam had seen what you two were doing, she would have thrown you off Dicapl. Stay away from Darrin if you know what's good for you."

Miss Pucket questioned, "Do I detect a note of jealousy in your voice?"

Jealousy has nothing to do with it. I'm on Sprite Security, and it's my job to report to Moonbeam what you two were doing and show her the pictures I took of you and Darrin a short while ago."

Miss Puckett remained silent, lowered her head and said, "It looks like you have me over the proverbial barrel, so, yes, I will stay away from Darrin."

"Good, I won't report the incident between you and Darrin to my boss, Sprite Moonbeam. But if she hears about it, I'll say it slipped my mind."

Once Misty flew away, Moe caught Miss Pucket's attention and said, "Purity in any relationship is a must, but snuggling in a warm blanket with your man in front of a crackling fire is the way to go."

"Your point is?"

"Stay away from getting into it in the jungle because you may pick up an insect bite on your tushy that you won't want. Darrin unknowingly became engaged to Sprite Misty. He tried to explain to her that it was a mistake, but she is not listening and would have the head of any woman who stood between her and Darrin.

"Understood. Sprites are a force to be reckoned with, and I do not want to tangle with them. So, I'll see you later,"

Moe then searched the garden for an herb that would speed up the healing of Tina's bad wing when she found a woman's left arm. She picked it up, studied it, and thought, "I wonder if this is Ruthie's? Because she's always losing things." Moe then froze, ready for action, when a hand grabbed the back of her blouse. Before she could react, she heard a male voice say, "There you are, Moe. Have you seen my Little Princess Tina?"

"No, I haven't. Try the cafeteria."

Moe then asked, "I found this in the bushes. What do you think,"

"It may belong to Ruthie," stated Sentinel-One.

Sentinel One then asked, "Did you hear that moan?"

"I sure did, and I think it came from those bushes." Stated Moe.

Sentinel One parted the large fiery red bush, and there was a disheveled Ruthie holding her left leg in one arm. Sentinel One helped her to a bench, put her arm and leg back on, and questioned, "You wanna tell me why you were hiding with an arm and a leg off?"

"Alex did this to me and tried to drag me back to Earth. So I stole Patsy's portal remote, pushed a few buttons, and wound up here all a mess."

Sentinel One helped a disheveled Ruthie to the Infirmary so the Doctor could analyze her to see if everything was working in order before she released her.

Mandy, a five-foot-five-inch woman with short light brown hair and a deep blue sundress, entered the Infirmary and asked, "Doc, I heard the new Mandroid; Ruthie got herself in a peck of trouble. Would you mind if I lend a hand?"

"Thank you for the offer, but you don't have any experience in the medical field or know anything about Mandroids."

"I know more about Mandroids than anyone, and showed the doctor her qualifications, then said, "Now let me see Ruthie."

A shocked Doc Stevenson stated, "Sure, be my guest,"

Mandy entered Ruthie's alcove in the Infirmary, handed her a mug of herbal tea, and said, "You need to rest and get yourself together before you do anything else. Because you have been through a lot this past week, I'll have Debbie, Sam, and Tippy's adopted daughter, Deltan bring you and Tina to the hot springs and stand guard while you relax."

With Sprite Tina and Ruthie soaking in the hot springs, Darrin walked out of the Omega One Headquarters building, down the mountain road halfway, and entered the jungle on the left side of the road for two hundred yards. Alex approached Darrin and asked, "Do you have the Sprite and the woman for me yet?"

"I'm having a hard time because of Sentinel One and that feisty little Sprite Tina."

An angry Alex stated, "I want to add Mandroid Ruthie and Patsy to the others I already have so I can take them through the vortex and present them to Queen Victoria. Oh, and don't forget Sprite, Tina,"

"I'm doing my best, Sir."

"You're an Ace Detective on Earth, so track them down, then drag their sorry bodies to me, and I don't care if you have to kill them. I want them."

"I'm not gonna kill someone just because they're a runaway." Stated Darrin.

"Look, Detective, I paid you good money to track down Ruthie and Tina and bring them back to me. Because if you don't, I'll have your sorry hide nailed on my living room wall. Now, do your job!"

"What crime have they committed that you want them back dead or alive?"

"Ruthie was one of my experiments that I was going to give to Queen Victoria, but she escaped, and I don't want her to know that she has the strength of 15 men,"

"What about Sprite Tina? She's just a little bit of a thing and means no harm to anyone,"

"Because of me, that little Sprite can do amazing things, and I want them under my control. If I can't have it, I'll have them buried six feet under. Now do what you were hired to do,"

Darrin quietly made his way to the hot springs carefully studied Ruthie and Tina, opened a portal to a jungle planet, and the fierce Jaguar slowly crept through and approached the Hot Springs.

Darrin slowly opened the gate to the hot springs, allowing the Jaguar to enter with its head lowered, growling.

Sprite Tina jumped out of the hot water and slowly made her way to the ferocious cat, humming a soft tune. The cat growled and slashed at Tina, but she continued to approach, humming. She then put her hand towards the cat and stated in a soft voice, "It's alright, Kitty, no one is going to hurt you."

The fierce animal's countenance softened, and began to purr. Tina petted the cat's head and rolled over on its back with its feet up. She climbed on the cat's stomach and scratched it. She then motioned to Debbie to get something to tie the cat.

Wild Debbie led the cat away. Ruthie approached Tina and stated in a harsh voice, "You could have gotten yourself killed by doing a stupid stunt like that."

"I don't think so. I had this inner feeling that if I hummed a soft tune, the cat would quiet down, and it did. I might be honest with you: Alex had me locked in a cage in his laboratory, experimenting on me. My ability to calm a wild beast is one of the things Alex gave me. The other thing is I can open a portal to other dimensions. If you excuse me, I'm getting back into that soothing water until I look like a prune."

"Taming a kitty cat is no problem, but you don't have any defense if a guy barged through that gate and wanted to use the Hot Springs and saw us naked. I mean, there are no alarms, sensors, or nothing to warn us that a bunch of guys are on their way."

Tina stated, "This is off limits to all men, so no need to worry."

Ruthie stated, "While you were taking care of the cat, I scouted around and found a pair of men's footprints. So I suggest we get dressed before he sees us like this."

Darrin quietly approached the hot springs to capture Ruthie and Tina and was about to open the gate when he spotted Debbie approaching. He quickly ducked behind a large bush and quietly crept back to the Omega One Headquarters without being seen.

Ruthie walked up to Debbie and stated, "The other day, I overheard Betty Elizabeth Tartan talking to one of her friends that while she was using the hot springs a few days ago, she had a personal encounter with Darrin and is concerned that she may be pregnant."

All the men at the Omega One Headquarters have been warned that they are not to be caught within a mile of the Hot Springs at any time. So I'll approach Betty and Get the facts from her, and if it's true, there'll be an investigation, and Darrin will be prosecuted to the full extent of the law

9

The Escape

Misty, clad in forest green apparel with her face and hands smeared with green makeup, was perched high in a mango tree, watching Darrin's every move. When Miss Puckett approached Darrin outside at the back of the Omega One Headquarters, she hovered just behind Darrin and drew back her bow, saying, "He's mine, you cheap Hassie! So back off before you get an arrow in you."

Vilma picked up a rock and threw it at Misty, hitting her on the arm, saying, "Get out of here, you crazy halfwit Sprite!"

Misty dropped several feet after being struck by the rock, then flew up in a nearby tree. Vilma glanced around to ensure no one was watching, put her arms around Darrin, and kissed him several times.

Misty took careful aim and let an arrow fly striking Miss Puckett in her left butt cheek. Vilma let go a squeal, pulled the arrow out, and screamed, "Listen here, you little pest, if I ever get my hands on you, I'll beat you within an inch of your life! And I'll keep seeing Darrin as much as I want, and you will not stop me!"

Vilma gave Darrin a passionate kiss on his lips, saying, "I should go see Doc Chrissy and have my bottom bandaged, but I'll be back." and left.

Misty flew to Darrin and got in his face, saying, "You, Mister, belong to me. So stay away from that cheap floozy Miss Vilma Puckett."

"What in the world are you babbling about, you crazy Sprite? I never promised to marry you, so bother someone else for a change."

An angry Misty said, "OK, I'll spell it out so a dumb human like you will understand. "Do you remember when you bought me a big juicy at the diner? You then escorted me to my place and had me remove my top so you could take care of my big itchy. In the Sprite society, when a male Sprite wants his lady friend to get bare-chested in front of him after he buys her something, he is saying that he is seriously interested in her."

Darrin interrupted by saying, "I did those things just to be nice to you, and I couldn't let you suffer when you had a serious problem with your back."

"Hello, dumb human, you knew what it meant by me taking off my blouse in front of you, and I told you what it meant by us making out on the couch while I was bare-chested. When we kissed, that told me that you were seriously considering me to be my mate. When we crawled into bed together, I told you that it meant that you wanted to be my mate. You understood what it meant and we got into sex all that night. The result of that night with you, my future mate, is that I'm going to have your baby. Then, when you started to fool around with Miss Vilma Puckett, that was like slapping me in the face and giving me the right to fight for the father of my baby."

Darrin asked, "How do I know you didn't set me up so you could take me to court for child support for a baby that's not mine."

"Hello, dumb human. I already had a blood test by the Doctor, and the baby is half human and half Sprite, which means it's yours."

Darrin stated, "There are 250 men and women at Omega One headquarters. Out of that, 187 are married. That leaves somewhere around sixty-three single men you could have fooled around with. So back off before I have Tippy throw your little butt in jail for an assault with a deadly weapon."

"I am a jilted Sprite with the right to fight to have my mate back."

Darrin stated, "If you remember correctly, you wanted me to take care of your back problem and make out on your couch while you were half-dressed. Then you dragged me into your bedroom and began to fool around. So I just gave you what you wanted; if Tippy or Sam questions me, I will tell them that it was you who tripped me into getting into it with you because you wanted alimony from me because of some human you made love with and didn't want any buddy to know."

"It's your word against mine, and since I'm on Sprite Security, they will believe me rather than you off-worlder."

Darrin smiled, saying, "Hello, you dimwitted Sprite; I am Detective Darrin Duguay of Earth, and when the powers that be read my clean record and all my accomplishments, your goose is cooked. So get out of my face, you pesty insect, before I swatch you like a bug and deem it self-defense because you tried to shoot me with an arrow the way you did, Velma."

Misty hung her head, flew back to her place, resigned from her job security, and packed her clothes to move back to her home planet.

Ruthie politely knocked on Misty's door and hollered, "Anybody to home?"

A discouraged Misty greeted Ruthie, saying, "Hi, I'm glad you came when you did because I quit my job on Sprite Security and was about to return to my home on HP 5."

Ruthie stared at a dejected Misty and said, "Darrin isn't worth it because plenty of male Sprites out there would give their lives just to have a date with you."

"But I'm pregnant with Darrin's baby."

Ruthie stared at the sorrowful Sprite and said, "News flash, Misty. Humans and Sprites are incompatible, so you are not expecting Darrin's baby."

"It's not fair. I have fallen in love with Darrin since he bought me that big juicy and took care of the itch between my wings."

Ruthie then inquired, "Truthfully, was Darrin the one who suggested to take care of that itch between your wings, or was it you?"

"I did hint to him about how uncomfortable I felt with the itchy between my wings. But it was Darrin who suggested that I strip to my waist. I went into the bedroom so we could have more room. When he finished, my back felt so good that I gave him a kiss. Darrin continued kissing me; the next thing I knew, he was going for a home run. I could not stop him because he was so aggressive. Then, when Darrin bought me the fabulous morning meal, he was actually telling me that he was my mate. Yes, when a male and a female Sprite are serious in their relationship, the female Sprite gets bare chested In front of the one she is serious about. That way, she is actually telling him that she wants him for her mate. If Sprite walks away without any response, he turns her down. But if the Sprite responds affectionately, he says yes, we are to be together. But, if the male Sprite asked to see her bare chest, he is proposing to her, and at the time of intimacy, that's an agreement that they are mate, or as you humans would say, husband and wife. But to make the relationship binding and long-lasting, they must share their vows with a pastor."

Ruthie stated, "I think it's a case of miscommunication and cross signals. Darrin was trying to be nice to you by buying that juicy and helping you with the itch on your back. You thought he was coming on to you and was interested in you as a mate, and the whole thing wound up to be a big mess."

A female sprite with yellow hair, thirty-six inches tall, stuck her head in the front door and asked, "Misty, you got a minute?"

"Sure, come on in, Moonbeam. What's up?"

"I just reviewed your notice about quitting, and I'm here to tell you it's unacceptable. You are one of my top sprites in security, and you can't walk out on me like that."

"I suppose you heard about Darrin and me the other night and how I shot Velma with an arrow. And you heard from Darrin how everything was my fault. So because of that, I quit my job, and I'm going back to my home on HP 5 because I blew the Omega One Headquarters rules big time when I got in bed with Darrin when I shouldn't have."

"Your interactions with Darrin will be in your permanent file. But what I want you to do is to go undercover and find out what Darrin is up to. Because he's been seen hanging around that moral character, Alex, he may be into some hot water up to his neck and doesn't realize it, but I was hoping you could find out what's going on between him and Alex. Ohh, one more thing: When interacting with Darrin, keep your clothes on."

Misty giggled, then stated, "You mean I can't walk around my house naked and make out on my couch when Darrin is in my home for coffee or fellowship?"

"Definitely not, Misty." Stated Moonbeam forcefully.

"Ah shucks, I was hoping to invite Darrin over this evening so he could give me a body rub after we took a shower together." Misty then fell on the floor laughing because socializing is not one of her strong points.

Later that day, Ruthie approached Darrin in the Galaxy Diner, enjoying a burger with French fries, and sat in the booth across from him. She took off her left arm, swatted him on the head with it, then reattached it, saying, "What's the big idea taking that creep Alex's side?"

Darrin nodded; Alex walked up to Ruthie, sat next to her in the booth, and said, "If you cry out or try to run, I'll short-circuit you right here, and nobody will even know what happened. Now come with me and Darrin quietly, and you won't get hurt. We will stand and walk out the door slowly as if we are close friends. I repeat, one wrong move and someone in this diner will die."

Ruthie whispered as she left the diner with Alex, "You will not get away with this, that I promise you."

Sometime later, in the jungle, Alex parted a mass of tangled vines and entered some of the old ruins of Odessa, then shoved Ruthie on the debris-laden floor. Grabbed her upper right thigh, pushed it in rotated her leg upwards, and took it off so she couldn't escape.

Ruthie shouted, "Hey, watch where you are putting your hands, you pervert!"

Alex leaned Ruthie against a far wall and sat on her left, saying, "I am not going to hurt you; I just have to check your inner workings to ensure is everything functioning properly. He glanced at Darrin, saying, "Go outside to ensure no one followed us."

With Darrin gone, Alex sat behind Ruthie, unzipped the back of her dress, and said, "Don't worry. I'm not going to get fresh with you. I need to check the rotator cuffs on your arms and vertebrae to see if they're aligned correctly."

"Well, OK, but just watch where you put your hands." Stated a defensive Ruthie.

While Alex was rubbing his right hand up and down her shoulders, he quickly slid his left hand down her chest and pushed her left breast turning her off. He then lay her on a stainless steel table on her back and removed her clothes, her other leg and both arms, then put a white sheet over her nude body.

A panicky Ruthie opened her eyes and asked, "What are you gonna do to me?"

Alex let go of a sinister laugh and stated, "Somewhere on Dicapl, I have hidden the Mandroids, Softy Mullens, Jeff Stearns, and Terrie Joan Ramsey. All I need to do is capture Alice Birdson and Tom Marks. Then I can bring you all to Queen Victoria."

"What about Patsy Mullens? Did you catch her too?"

"Not yet, but I will."

"What are you gonna do with us?"

"The Galaxy will call me a genius and bow before me when I give the Mandroids to Queen Victoria so she can put her plan into action. Now shut up so I can concentrate, you conglomerate of computer circuits."

Thinking her fate was sealed, Ruthie closed your eyes and prayed that her death would be swift. She heard a little voice saying, "It's me, Tina, and Misty. We're crouched behind your head; let us know when Alex isn't looking so we can get you outta here."

Ruthie whispered, "You two Sprites are going to get yourself killed. Now get outta here before Alex sees you."

"Just let us know when Alex isn't looking. That's all we ask," stated Tina

"OK, if you insist on getting yourselves killed, Alex has his back to you and is busy working on his computer,"

Misty shot straight up in the air and let go of a high-pitched shriek. Then said, "Can't catch me," and darted off.

As soon as Alex took chase, Tina pushed a lamp over, tripping Alex. Misty spun around and dropped a piece of heavy debris on his head, knocking him out. Then yanked off Ruthie's bed sheet saying, "Woah, a naked Mandroid," and the two Sprites reattached Ruthie's limbs. Ruthie put on her clothes as Tina shouted, "We gotta get out of here before Darrin and Alex come too!"

Ruthie, Tima, and Misty raced outside and into the jungle just as Alex and Darin revived.

10

Escape

Ruthie held the two sprites in her arms as she raced through the jungle, hoping to escape Alex and Darrin. Some two hundred yards in, Alex caught up to Ruthie and fired his energy pistol, striking her left leg sending her tumbling to the ground, sending Tina and Misty flying through the air. Suddenly, a tall woman in a lacey blue dress with soft, wavy, light brown hair appeared in front of Ruthie and the two sprites. She quickly stretched out her right hand, creating an energy barrier between them, and said, "I am Ariana the Mighty, and you shall not pass."

"Out of the way, woman, that Mandroid and Sprite belong to me!" shouted Alex.

"All you want them for is to turn them into something inhuman then give them to the evil Victoria. Now back off," Ariana stated, pointing her right hand towards a tall tree. A blast of energy shot out of her hand, striking the tree and turning it to powder. She then pointed her hand toward Alex and Darrin and said, "Back off; you two will be next." Then, she blasted a hole two feet in diameter in front of Darrin and Alex.

Darrin stated, "You can keep your money, Alex. I'm outta here."

Alex said, "Lady, you don't know who you are dealing with. Now, hand over the Mandroid and the Sprite, and you won't get hurt."

Ariana transported Ruthie and the two sprites back to Omega One Headquarters dropped the energy barrier, stood a foot in front of Alex, and said, "You will also release the other Mandroids you have hidden." Then turned to walk away.

As soon as Ariana was fifty feet away, Alex shot her in the back with his energy pistol, hoping to kill her.

Ariana slowly turned around and quickly stretched out her arms towards Alex, sending him flying backward one hundred feet before hitting the ground. Then, she bellowed, "You will leave Ruthie and Tina alone and release the other Mandroids, or you will have me to deal with. Is that clear?" Alex then vanished.

At the Omega One Headquarters, Ariana approached Sam in the cafeteria, saying, "You have got to do something about Alex. He has captured all the Mandroids and is after Ruthie and Patsy."

"I'll get on it right away."

Ariana stated, "One more thing. I know when Alex put Ruthie's brain inside that Android body. However, I think she took something from him when she escaped from his lab. Why else would he be so vicious about getting her back?"

"I'll immediately put the Omega Force on that, thank you. Oh, and enjoy a cup of coffee on me."

Sentinel One casually scrolled in the cafeteria, grabbed himself a cup of hot coffee and spotted Ariana shitting in a booth by herself. He sat in the booth opposite her and said, "I can't thank you enough for rescuing Ruthie and the two sprites from Alex."

"I've tried to catch Alex in the past, but he's a slippery little bugger and has places to hide that I know not of. But one of these days, I will catch him and bring him to justice for all the garbage he's been causing throughout this galaxy."

"Would you like to drop by my place later cause I want to talk to you about things that lot of ears should not be hearing."

An hour later, in Sentinel One's home, he made a pot of coffee, handed Ariana her mug, and stated, "I'm very close friends with a cute little sprite named Tina, and I'm concerned that she may have feelings for me. What is your opinion?"

"I think Sprite and humans can be close friends or marry, and there have been rare occasions where a female sprite has given birth to a baby fathered by a human. I've checked with Misty, and she is pregnant by Darren. But that's not why you called me here, is it,"

Sentinel One took a swallow of his coffee and stated, "A day or two ago, Sprite Tina and I were searching for Alex when we were attacked. Tina was injured, so we took shelter in a cave. I took off Sprite Tina's clothes to tend to all her wounds. I feel guilty because I had to massage her little body before tending to her many wounds all over her. I then had to sleep with her in my briefs because I couldn't put her clothes back on because of the severity of her injuries. However, my body heat did keep her warm."

Ariana took a swallow of her coffee and asked, "What is it you are not telling me,"

Sentinel One swallowed nervously and said, "In the morning, we, ah, ah, you know."

"I won't know unless you tell me."

"I gave in to Tina's promptings because she was quite kittenish, and had just finished making love to Tina when Sprite Kayli flew into the cave and caught us and have been feeling guilty ever since."

"Tina may be just over three feet tall, but she is all woman and knows when a man is coming on to her. So she encouraged you all the more by being kittenish. Oh, and if Tina didn't want to curl up against your bare chest in the buff, she wouldn't have. And it was her who wanted sex, not you, so don't go blaming yourself."

"How do you know that."

"I've known Tina for years, and she can be a bit kittenish around men."

"Oh, one more thing. Alex is just a flunky. There's someone sinister who defies the description behind the scenes. Capturing the Mandroid is only the tip of the iceberg. What the queen wants to do with them, I don't know, but we have to find those other androids and keep Ruthie and Patsy from being captured at all costs.

Sentinel One intently studied Ariana and said, "You don't look too good."

"I feel fine. There is nothing wrong with me, so if you excuse me, I have got to go.

Sentinel One handed Ariana a thermometer, saying put this in your mouth."

"No, I feel great now. Respect my boundaries."

"Humor me and put this in your mouth,"

Some three minutes later, Sentinel One read the thermometer 102.5 and showed it to Ariana, saying, "You young Lady are not going anywhere. So take your clothes off, get in bed, and stay there. Because if you don't, this is gonna go higher, and it will kill you.

Ariana put her hand on her forehead, saying, "On second thought, you're right. I don't feel good. Could you please help me to the bedroom?"

In the bedroom, Sentinel One assisted Ariana in getting her clothes off and into a pair of his pajamas. Then he put his arm around her and helped her into bed. He sat in a chair by the bed, saying, "I'm not going anywhere until you're better."

When Ariana's temperature rose to 103.1, showed it to her and stated, "I need to give you a cold body rub down to lower your temperature."

An angry Ariana stated firmly, "Against my better judgment, I let you see me in my undies so you could help me with my PJs. But I refuse to let you see me naked for a rub down."

"I have to give you a cold rubdown in order to lower your temperature."

"I said no because all you want to do is to get your sexual jollies at my expense."

"Okay, but if I don't give you a cold rub down, your fever will reach 107, then you will die, and that's a fact."

Ariana relented, saying, "On second thought, I changed my mind." Then felt nervous and squeamish as she took off her pajamas and underwear and lay on the bed naked. Ariana then moaned nervously as Sentinel One took a cold pan of water and a washcloth and wiped her arms, stomach, and legs. He then turned her over and wiped her back down to her feet. He assisted her with her pajamas and helped her back in bed, saying, "Now that wasn't so bad. But this I know you are going to get through this; I promise you."

Ariana stated in protest, "Did you have to wipe me down there? I mean, really, Sentinel One."

"To bring your fever down, yes I did,"

Some two days later, Sentinel One took Ariana's temperature, which wasn't any lower than 102, and gave Ariana another wipe-down with her protesting. He slapped her bare butt saying, "Settle down or I'll turn you over my knee and spank you."

"Oh, you would love doing that." And remain silent.

Some three days later, he smiled and said, "Well, it looks like another day or two, and you'll be up and running around as usual."

A kittenish Ariana studied Sentinel One's movements and asked, "When was the last time you had some sleep,"

"About five days ago. Why?"

She pulled back the covers and patted the mattress next to her, saying, "You need your rest."

Ariana smiled devilishly as Sentinel-One stripped to his briefs and crawled into bed with her. She put her arm on his chest, placed her head on his bare shoulder, saying, "This is more like it," and drifted off to sleep.

Sentinel One was fixing the morning meal the next day when Ariana approached him in her PJs and he growled, "You didn't respect my wishes this morning. Because you wanted to get into touchy-feely that would have led to something wrong according to the Word of God. Now eat your morning meal,"

Ariana wrapped her arms around Sentinel One and was kissing him when Tina flew in the door. She saw Ariana coming onto Sentinel One, paused, and stated in anger, "Ariana, finish your coffee, dress, and go." Tina stared at Sentinel One and said, "We have a problem." She looked at Ariana, still in her PJs, and said, "Do you mind? I want to talk to Sentinel One alone."

After Ariana dressed and left, Tina sat on the comfortable blue sofa in the living room and patted the cushion next to her.

Sentinel One sat on her right and questioned, "Is there something wrong,"

"Yes, it's about you and me."

Sentinel One asked, "Oh, did I do something wrong?"

"Remember when we were in the cave?"

"Yes, we got super friendly with each other, and I am sorry I did that."

Tina giggled and said, "No problem. However, you saw me bare-naked, feeding me, and sleeping with me, and the copulation we did that morning means you are my mate. Yes"

"Do you have a bun in the oven?"

"No. But I am willing to fight for you."

Silence ruled for two minutes before Tina looked at the blue rug on the floor and said, "I ah, set you up because I need someone to protect me from Alex."

Sentinel One silently stared at Tina for a minute, held her in his arms, tenderly kissed her lips, and then stated, "I want you to take a shower, then get in my bed and get some rest."

"But I'll have to sleep in just my step-ins."

"So big deal, you are my wife."

"You mean you accept me as your mate?" questioned a surprised Tina.

"Yes, I do."

Tina gave Sentinel One a kiss and flew into the bathroom for her shower.

Several hours later, Sentinel One was cleaning up the kitchen when he heard a commotion from the bedroom. He entered the bedroom and saw Alex climbing out the window with Sprite Tina in his arms. He raced out the back door, Leveled his energy pistol at him, shouted, "Drop the Sprite!" and fired a shot over his head.

Alex dropped Tina on the ground and disappeared into the jungle.

Sentinel One took off his shirt, put it around Tina to cover her exposed body, and asked, "Are you alright?"

"Yeah, I think so. But next time something like this happens, tell him to put me down." Tina flew skyward, pointed, and said, "I see some birds flying up out of the jungle northwest of here; that's where Alex is heading."

Sentinel One grabbed his three-o-three rifle from over the fireplace and headed northwest with Tina flying overhead.

Some 30 minutes later, Sentinel One spotted Alex and fired a shot over his head, saying, "Halt or the next bullet will be in your head."

"You wouldn't dare shoot an unarmed man," stated Alex.

"Don't push your luck, and it won't happen. Now, why are you so vehemently after Ruthie and Tina."

"They're mine because I created them in my lab, and I want them back,"

"I don't care if they were born in your lab or not; you don't own any human being or Sprite. Besides, Tina is now my mate, my wife, and don't even think of coming close to her, or there won't be enough left of you to scrape up and bury. Now, you're returning with me to Omega One Headquarters and stand trial for all the garbage you have done."

With Alex behind bars at the Omega One Headquarters, he stated, "Queen Victoria hired me to create Ruthie and Tina and she won't like the fact that you stole them from me."

Sentinel One grabbed Alex's shirt, pulled it, slammed his face against the bars, and asked, "Tell me what the queen wants with them."

Alex laughed, then said, "Yeah, right, not on your life."

"Then tell me why the queen is blocking out our sun,"

"When she thinks you've suffered enough in the dark and cold, she'll state her terms," He stared at Tippy standing on Sentinel One's right and stated, "And you, Tippy, don't even think about firing up the Alfa Wing and investigate the planet blocking out the sun because you won't get 5 feet."

Later, Tina sat on Sentinel One's shoulder as he walked to the beach. Spotted Ruthie leisurely lying on a dark green blanket in a pale skimpy yellow bathing suit. He approached her, knelt, and then questioned, "What did you steal from Alex,"

"Nothing, except this stupid contraption he calls a Mandroid. Why don't you ask him what he stole from me, like my body."

Sentinel One put Tina down and said, "Do everyone a favor and put some clothes on because not everybody wants to see your bare derriere."

11

Convicted

Sentinel One put Tina on his shoulders, walked along the beach, and met Mandy coming out of the jungle. She was clad in a cute red bikini, accentuating her athletically toned figure. She smiled at Sentinel One and asked, "Have they figured out why there is an object blocking the sun?"

Mandy's smile had an almost hypnotic effect on Sentinel One as he stated, "

"Queen Victoria is ticked off at us about something and wants to make us suffer before he gives us she ultimatum."

Sentinel One then studied Mandy's physically toned figure, glanced at Tina, and smiled.

As Mandy was walking away, Tina whispered in his ear, "Go after her."

"But I am married to you, so I can't,"

"The marriage between a human and a Sprite is frowned upon in the Sprite community, and we haven't gone to a minister with a marriage license to make it acceptable in the human community."

"Are you sure you want me to catch up to Mandy?"

"Yes, now go after her before she gets away,"

As Sentinel One caught up to Mandy, Tina took her communicator out of her pocket and said, "This is Little Flee. Sentinel One checks out good so far, but we should send him to Earth with Mandy to check out Alex's connections there. That will tell us if he is on the up and up. Tina out,"

Tears silently rolled down Tina's cheeks as she realized, "What have I done? I just sent my mate, my love, into the arms of another woman, and I don't think I'll get him back."

A short time later, Sprite Tina casually entered the cafeteria with her head down, saw Greg, approached the table, and said, "Greg, I'm glad to see you back home again. Are you going to stay longer than a couple of days now? And who is this with you,"

"This is Kimmy from Earth,"

Kimmy waved as she smiled, saying, "It's so nice to meet you, Tina,"

Tina gave Kimmy a hug, saying, "Can you tell me all about Earth because I've never been there,"

"Of course, I'll tell you about Earth. We have these things called oceans, which are basically giant bodies of water that cover most of the planet, and there are so many different kinds of animals, like elephants and lions. Well, I guess you guys probably know all about cats since you seem to have an infinite of them

Kimmy froze mid-sentence, staring at the wide-eyed lion quietly strolling into the cafeteria and up to Kimmy purring, licked her hand, then left. She laughed in amazement in question, "That was surreal. What kind of a creature is he,"

"That was General the Security Lion on loan from the Galaxy Sentinel. By him licking your hand, you meet his approval."

"His fur felt so soft,"

Sam, also known as Alpha One, approached Greg, studied Kimmy, and stated, "I'm in charge of the Alpha Squadron, and I want you three on the team. Ma'am, I believe you have a gift that we desperately need. Could you please follow me to the gym?"

Feeling honored and slightly intimidated, Kimmy stood up, saying, "I'll do what I can to help."

Sam pointed to some barbells in the gym and said, "Let's see how high you can lift that."

Kimmy reluctantly took hold of the barbells and easily lifted them over her head in astonishment. Giggled, then said, "I guess I'm stronger than I thought,"

Sam said with the barbells back on the gym floor, "You just picked up 1000 lbs. with ease. How would you like to be called Kimmy, also known as Kimmy the Strong?" Then, Sam handed Kimmy a broad-brimmed hat, a cape, and a crystalline broad sword and said, "Don't worry. We'll show you how to use them. Now get ready for a life of adventure."

"Kimmy the Strong, that sounds so cool. I'll do my best to live up to the title." She took the hat, Cape, and sword and looked at them wonderfully.

Sam stared at Tina and said, "Let me see you fly around the gym."

Some forty-five seconds later, Tina asked, "How was that?"

"A turtle could have gone faster." Sam knelt, stared at Tina, and said, "This is what I want you to do. Concentrate on being at this spot while you were flying."

Tina did as Sam instructed, and it only took a second to fly around the gym this time. She stared at Sam in astonishment, saying, "Wow! I didn't know I could fly that fast. Thanks."

Sam looked down at her and said, "Tina, also known as Tina the Swift."

"Tina the Swift, I like that name, Tina then hollered, "Watch out, Tina the Swift is coming through!"

Sam gazed at Greg and said, "Anyone brave enough to marry a woman as strong as Kimmy has to be brave so you'll be known as Greg or Zeta the Brave."

Sometime later, Greg was resting on the white sandy beach of Crater Lake with Kimmy, wearing a cute red and white bikini, and asked, "What do you think of being here?"

"This is not what I expected. But I am happy to be here with you. But the last one in the water buys coffee for a week!" and took off for the water.

At the water's edge splashing, Kimmy, Greg glanced up and said, "It would be a lot better if the sun were out from behind that stupid planet or whatever it is in front of the sun."

Just then, a woman's scream echoed from the jungle. Greg said, "Come on, sweet, we should investigate, and the two of them ran into the jungle in search of whoever was in trouble.

Kimmy looked up and said, "It's impossible to find the one in trouble in that dense jungle."

At the edge of the jungle, Greg heard a growl coming from his left and said, "This way." He found Ariana on the ground with her legs under a fallen tree. He checked to see how she was and said, "We'll get you out of this."

Ariana stated, "I was walking through the jungle when I heard a noise, looked up, and would have been killed by this tree if it wasn't for my lightning-quick reflexes as I jumped out of its way."

Greg glanced at his wife and asked, "Babe, see if you can lift that tree,"

"Are you serious? That was a miracle that I lifted those weights in the gym; I can't lift that tree."

"If you lifted that barbell in the gym, you could do this. I want you to kneel by the tree as close as you can, put your hands underneath it, and see how high you can lift it."

Kimmy knelt by the tree, then let go a grown, and sent the tree flying fifty feet. She stared at it and said, "Hey, I am strong."

Greg was about to help Ariana up when a blast of energy from a laser rifle struck a tree nearby, sending him on top of her. He smiled sheepishly, rolled off her, tackled his wife, and said, "Stay down; that tree didn't fall by accident; someone cut it down to kill Ariana."

Kimmy clutched her chest behind a tree, saying, "That was close. Maybe we can sneak out or create a diversion,"

"You're strong, so why don't you throw that rock to our left, and we will run to our right,"

Kimmy took a deep breath and said, "Alright, On three, one, two, three," and threw a large rock. Greg helped Ariana to her feet, and the three of them darted to their right and made it safely back to the beach.

Greg turns to Kimmy and asks, "You okay?"

Trying to catch her breath, she stated, "That was insane, but I am okay; I think we should rest for a while."

"I couldn't agree with you more," and gave Kimmy a much-needed hug.

She snuggles into Greg's arms, feeling safe and protected, saying, "Thanks' Greg, I couldn't have done it without you."

Greg looked at Kimmy, saying, "Uh, sweet, I think you should change because you ripped the bottom half of your bikini pretty bad,"

Kimmy looked down, saying, "Oops, I guess I got carried away in the action."

"That's okay, your normal." Stated Greg.

Kimmy giggled softly, stood, brushed the sand off her, and said, "I'll go change real quick,"

"Do you know you have a cute tush," stated Greg, smiling.

Kimmy blushed as she looked over her shoulder at Greg before heading to the bathhouse to change.

Greg knelt by Ariana and asked, "How's your legs doing?"

"I think my right leg is broken."

As Kimmy exited the bathhouse, Greg hollered, "Sweet, see if there's a leg brace in the bathhouse because I think Ariana broke her leg!"

She nodded, searched through the first stage supplies, rushed outside, hollering, "Found it!" and hurried to Greg with it.

"Sweet, lift Ariana's leg gently so I can put the brace on her."

Kimmy knelt beside Ariana and carefully lifted the injured leg, saying, "Here you go, Greg."

Greg helped Ariana to her feet, saying, "No rest for the tired. We have to get Ariana to the infirmary."

Once Ariana was in the infirmary, Greg led Kimmy into the Botanical Garden, which contained beautiful flowers from all over the galaxy. She stood in awe as she gazed at the alien floral arrangements, saying, "Everything here is so beautiful."

"Let's sit by those red fire bushes and rest a while." Stated Greg.

Kimmy smiled, sat down, and leaned her head on Greg's shoulder, saying, "That does sound nice,"

Greg put his arm around Kimmy's waist, kissed her, then asked, "Did you hear that? I think I heard someone moaning."

Kimmy blushed and leaned in, pressing her lips against Greg's lips softly

Greg's hand gently slid down Kimmy's back, paused, and said, "There it is again; I think someone is in those red fire bushes."

Kimmy pulled back slightly and asked, "Are you sure?"

Greg stated, "Whatever you were thinking of doing, put it on pause for a brief moment while I check," Greg parted the bushes and found Sprite Tina crying.

Instantly concerned, Kimmy stood, hurried to Tina, and asked, "What's wrong?"

Sobbing, Tina explained, "Sentinel One and I became mates or husband and wife, as you humans put it. I didn't think he loved me because I am a Sprite, so I sent him after Mandy. I realized what I did was foolish, but I'll never see him again now."

Kimmy put her arm around Tina, saying, "I had no Idea. But I'm sure Sentinel One cares about you deeply because you two were so close before."

Sobbing, Tina stated, "I told Tippy to send Sentinel One and Mandy to check out Alex's connections on Earth,"

A concerned Kimmy stated, "I didn't know. That means they're going to be in danger. Should we go for back up or call to ensure they're all right?"

Greg stated, "Tippy sent Mandy to Earth, and Sentinel One is in the cafeteria waiting for Tina,"

Kimmy looked at her husband and said, "You manipulated me into marrying you and brought me here."

A shocked and surprised Greg questioned, "What brought this on?"

"I was looking at our marriage license the other day, and it looks like it's a fraud."

"I assure you our marriage license is not a fake."

Feeling overwhelmed and angry, Kimmy hollered. "I need some space," and returned to the beach house.

Some three days later, Greg returns to the beach house and asks, "How are you doing, my Sweet?"

"Don't touch me; you made a huge decision without consulting me."

"The Alpha Wing is warming up, and we need to be there right now."

"I don't care. I am not going, and I want you to take me back to Earth now,"

"I can't do that because this is a top-secret installation, and you've seen too much, so I cannot bring you back to Earth with the attitude you have right now."

Kimmy shook her head slowly, saying, "I can't; I can't be with you on the Omega One team when you lied and manipulated me the way you did, and I trusted you."

"I didn't lie and manipulate you,"

In a firm tone of voice, Kimmy stated, "You did, and I can't forget what you did to me, so I need time to think,"

Tippy walked in, stared at Kimmy, saying, "I'm here to tell you that this is a top-secret installation, and I cannot allow you to go back to Earth because you would jeopardize the security of the planetary alliance,"

Kimmy stared at Tippy and asked, "What does that mean?"

"Like I just said, the Omega One Headquarters is a top-secret installation, and you're part of the team, and what you have seen means you cannot leave just like that, especially with your attitude."

"I can't stay here. I'm going back to Earth whether you like it or not,"

Tippy ordered, "Security, lock Kimmy up on the charges of conspiracy,"

Kimmy desperately struggled against the guards, hollering, "Let me go, let me go! I won't say anything, I promise!"

Kimmy broke free and darted toward the door but before she could open it Tippy stunned her with her energy pistol.

In jail, at the Omega One headquarters, Kimmy sobbed, saying, "Please, Greg, Get Me Out of here,"

"I can't. Remember, I'm a liar and a manipulator,"

With tears streaming down her face, Kimmy said, "I take it all back. Please Get Me Out of here."

Greg returned to the jail a week later and saw Kimmy lying on a small cot in a cell, curled up in a ball with a blanket around her, and she said with tears in her eyes, "Go away,"

"How about a hug?"

Kimmy shuddered and turned her back to Greg, saying, "No, please leave me alone."

A somber Tippy approached, saying, "Greg, you can take her for her last walk,"

Kimmy stepped out of her cell, looked at the facility's sterile walls, and asked, "Where are we going?"

"To the gas chamber,"

Fear jolted Kimmy's system as she screamed, "The what?"

"The gas chamber; these guards will take you there."

A panic-stricken Kimmy struggled against the guards, screaming, "No, no, please, I'm sorry!"

The guards left Greg alone with Kimmy in a white sterile room and asked, "Would you like a hug?"

Kimmy shook her head no, then said, "Tell me that you were going to put me in the gas chamber. Why would you even joke about something like that?"

"It's no joke the guards gave us some time to be alone together. But they're back. Kimmy trembled in fear as she stared at the gas chamber door, unable to speak. She then struggled against the restraining straps as the guards Russell to strap her into the chair in the gas chamber, pleading, "No, no, please."

Just as the gas was released into the chamber, Tippy rushed into the room and stopped the execution.

Kimmy breathed a sigh of relief and said, "Thank you, thank you." Kimmy then collapsed in Greg's arms, trembling, and clung tightly to him. Greg turned to Tippy and questioned, "Is it alright if I bring Kimmy back to my place for a day or two?"

"Yes,"

Kimmy lifted her head and smiled at him, saying, "Thank you, Greg,"

In Greg's home at the Omega One Headquarters, Greg brought Kimmy to his bedroom and said, "Why don't you get some rest,"

Kimmy stared at the unfamiliar surroundings and said, "I don't think I can sleep," and pulled away from Greg.

"Why can't you sleep?"

"I, I need space, some time to think,"

When Greg kissed Kimmy's neck, she stiffened slightly, but Greg kept kissing her. She pushed Greg's hand away and turned her back as Greg tugged on her clothes. She then stated, "Not now, Greg. I'm not ready for that right now." She turned to face Greg, stared into his eyes, and asked, "Are you sure you still want to be with me after everything that's happened?"

"Yes, I do,"

With tears streaming down her face, Kimmy said softly, "I guess I do too." Kimmy slipped into her white tank top and underwear, put her hair in a ponytail, yawned, and crawled into bed with Greg.

12

The truth revealed

Early the next morning, Tippy knocked on Greg's front door. Kimmy answered in her long, pink, fuzzy robe and slippers, yawned and then asked, "Hey, Tippy. What's up?"

"Doc Chrissy Stevenson wants to see you in her office as soon as possible."

Clad in jeans and a black shirt, Greg handed Tippy a green mug of coffee and asked, "Why does the Doc want to see Kimmy?"

"She didn't say. Oh, the Alpha Wing is warming up as we speak."

"What's the mission?"

"To see what we can do about removing the object blocking the sun."

In Doc Stevenson's office, she had Kimmy sit on the exam table with a Jhonny coat on. She then checked her heart and lungs. Then, she had her lie down on the exam table and put a wet cloth over her eyes, halting all of Kimmy's movements.

Doc Stevenson said to Greg, "Put your hand on your wife's bare stomach."

Greg did and asked, "Okay, now what?"

"Do you feel the warmth of her body?"

"Yeah, so what,"

"That means there is something wrong because she's not supposed to be that hot."

"You mean she has a fever?" questioned Greg.

"No. Your wife is an Android Humanoid and is malfunctioning,"

A puzzled Greg questioned, "A what?"

"Kimmy is a high-class Android Humanoid, and there is something wrong with her. Because that's why she is happy and loving one minute, then wants to be left alone at other times. I put a wet cloth over her eyes to shut her down until I can repair the damage."

Shocked over the news of what his wife really was, Greg stated, "You mean I married and had been intimate with a robot? No, I won't believe that nonsense."

The doctor slid a four-inch long by a quarter-inch broad probe in Kimmy's left ear and removed her face, revealing the inner workings of her head."

Greg screamed, "This is some kind of a sick joke!"

"It's no joke, Greg, this is who Kimmy really is."

"That's it, I'm out of here! I refuse to be linked to that pile of junk! I'll be on the Alpha Wing if you want me for anything else."

After Greg had stormed out of the office, the doctor removed the scalp and studied the almost human-looking brain. Then, she noticed the limbic system located underneath the cerebral cortex and above the brainstem had several shunts. She looked closer, saying, "Hello, what have we here?" She called her doctor colleague and sent him a picture of the shunts on Kimmy's brain, and he stated, "You're right. Those shunts should not be there. What you need to do is carefully cut the shunts, then dab some liquid plastic on the ends."

"Wouldn't it be easier if I remove them completely?"

"If you removed them, you're going to cause great damage to the brain, which means she'll be ready for the scrap heap."

After Doc Stevenson clipped the shunts around the limbic system, she cut a few more that dealt with memory and replaced the scalp and face. Kimmy sat up, looked around, and asked, "Where's my hubby Greg?"

"He's on the Alpha Wing."

"I need to see him right now. He slipped off the exam table and headed for the door.

Doc Stevenson asked, "Kimmy, don't you think you should put some clothes on before you leave my office?"

"Oh yeah, that would help, wouldn't it? Hey, the men won't mind seeing my bare posterior."

"Come back and get dressed," ordered Doc Stevenson sternly.

"Okay, sure. I was just kidding. I Would never expose myself in public."

As Kimmy dressed, Doc Stevenson asked, "Do you feel any different?"

"Come to think of it, I do. My memory is clear for the first time in a long while, and I have peace, meaning the battle of wanting to be alone and to push people away is gone."

Doc Stevenson paused for a few seconds, then asked, "Do you know who or what you are?"

"Yes. I am a top-of-the-line Android Humanoid. I have a full range of emotions, from love to hate. I can be passionate during intimacy with my husband, or I can scream bloody murder when someone does me wrong. I can even laugh at my husband's stupid jokes. My skin is smooth, and my breasts are soft and firm."

Doc Stevenson halted Kimmy, saying, "Thank you for your inventory, and I'm thankful you're back to normal. Do you know who messed up your brain?"

"Alex, he didn't want me to tell others that he's gonna give the Mandroids to evil Queen Victoria who will use them as her secret strike force. So he made me look like a basket case."

On the Alpha Wing, Kimmy slowly approached Greg, planted a gentle kiss on his right cheek, and said, "Hi, Sweet. You and I have to talk."

"Get away from me, you bucket of bolts?" and gave her a shove.

Kimmy quickly glanced around to make sure they were alone, smiled, and then asked in a soft voice, "Do you remember the first time we made love and how I responded? Did I act like a bucket of bolts, as you call me?"

"No, your actions and emotions were extremely intense, which blessed me."

"Do you remember the number of times we snuggled in front of the fireplace in our night clothes and how I acted?"

"Yes, I do. You are very loving, gentle, and compassionate in a way that I have never seen any woman act. But you're a robot."

"No, I'm an Android Humanoid, which is as close to a human as one can get. However, 40-50 years down the road, when you're old and wrinkly, I'll still have a young, shapely figure, and my breasts will still be firm and perky; in other words, I won't age. If you don't believe me, give me a hug and see for yourself."

Greg gave Kimmy a hug and then said, "True. You are soft and very loving, but that doesn't negate that you are a mechanical contrivance put together in some mad scientist's laboratory."

"Like I asked before. Did I act like a robot when you made love to me?"

Greg angrily stated, "Please don't remind me that I had an intimate relationship with a robot. Now go to your scanning post and get ready for takeoff."

The rest of the Omega Squadron entered the Alpha wing. Tippy sat in the command chair, saying, "Moe, take the pilot's chair. Debbie, take the copilot. Greg, you have the energy cannons. Epsil, you have the scanner. Moe, take us out."

On route to the object blocking the sun, Epsil stated, "The scanner is picking up two assault fighters coming at us super-fast!"

"I'm on it," shouted Greg.

The offer wing shook from the blast from the attacking fighters. Greg fired several blasts from the energy cannons, taking out one vessel. Moe swerved the alpha Wing starboard, spun around, and Greg fired another volley of energy blasts that took out the second attacking ship.

With the two enemy assault fighters destroyed, the Alpha wing approached the object blocking the sun.

Kimmy stated, "The scanner says there isn't anything there. Wait a minute. The scanner just picked up a round object three feet in diameter and is sending out alpha waves, creating a three-dimensional object the size of a moon in front of the sun."

"Can you jam that signal?"

"Give me a minute." Then shouted," Bingo!" when the object blocking the sun vanished. She then said, Greg, fire, and energy blast at these coordinates, "00125.5."

A small explosion shook the Alpha Wing. Kimmy then stated, "It's been destroyed. Then stated, "We may have our son back, but we should be prepared for another assault of some kind."

Back at Omega One Headquarters, Tippy approached Mandy in the cafeteria and said, "I want you and Greg to go to Chicago, Illinois, on Earth, and scope out Alex's cronies and take them out."

"Okay. We'll be ready to leave at two this afternoon."

"I'll have Debbie open a portal for the two of you."

Tina was crouched down in the booth nearby and sobbed when she saw Sentinel One give Mandy a hug and leave with her. She stared at the deep orange shirt she had for Sentinel One, threw it in the garbage, and went to find a quiet place to pray.

At two in the afternoon, Tina crawled out from under a large fire bush, glanced at her computer watch, and moaned, "He's gone to be with her, and I'll never see him again." She sat down and cried her eyes out for the loss of her mate, Sentinel One.

As Tina was crying, she caught the scent of flowers, grew dizzy, and passed out. Coming to hours later, she was in an old rusty cage in a rundown building clad in tattered rags that barely covered her little body. She saw Alex and shouted, "Hey, you there, Meat Head; where are my clothes?"

"Oh good, you're awake."

Tina bellowed again, "I asked where, are, my clothes you twisted piece of garbage,"

"You won't need them after your surgery." He then threw a few scraps of food in her cage.

Tina threw the food back at Alex, saying, "I'd rather starve to death than eat that putrefying stuff you call food."

Alex opened Tina's cage door and approached her, saying, "You are going to do what I say. Take off your clothes and lay on the stainless steel exam table in the middle of the room."

"Go suck and egg Creep. I don't get naked in front of strange men, and they don't come any stranger than you."

When Alex tried to forcefully take off Tina's clothes, she flew out of the cage and perched on the rugged chandelier hanging from the ceiling in the middle of the room, saying, "Can't catch me, Creep."

"Come down here and do what I say, Tina, or I won't give you any food for the next four days."

"Newsflash, Alex, I stopped being your puppet, reporting everything the Omega Squadron does." Tina, through her watch at Alex, said, "I will no longer be your Little Flea reporting to you everything the Omega Squadron does, and I will not be your little mistress anymore."

"Do you remember where I found you, Little Flee, and how you were living, and this is how you repay me?"

"Yeah, I know I was living in the swamps on Epsilon Prime, living on larvae, bugs, and Beatles. But to tell you the truth, Mr. Alex, I would rather eat the bugs, beetles, and larvae than eat the gross stuff you give me for food."

An electric shock suddenly coursed through Tina's little body, causing her to fall lifeless to the floor.

Sometime later, Tina came too, lying on her side in a soft bed dressed in a frilly, deep pink negligee. She didn't want to open her eyes because she was in bed with a strange man snuggled up to her back. Fearing that Alex had forced her into a life of prostitution, Tina's mind became crowded with thoughts about how she was going to escape. She then felt the man place his hand on her breast and thought, "Oh God no, I don't want to get into it sexually with this guy," She slowly opened her eyes, looked at the silver ring on the man's hand and shouted, "Sentinel One! You didn't go to Chicago with that cheap floozy?" spun around, and smothered him with kisses.

"Why would I do that when I am married to you."

"You mean you didn't go after Mandy?"

"We talked, but that's as far as it went."

Tina quickly removed her negligee, saying, "No more talk, I want you now."

The following day, Tina rolled over in bed, greeted her husband with a kiss, and said, "Thank you for a wonderful night. Now let me fix the morning meal."

As Tina took a sip of her chamomile tea while she sat at the table, she looked down and said, "Sweet, do you remember when we were attacked while searching for Alex? I, ah, was ordered by him to set a trap so he could kill you because you are a threat to his plan."

Emotionally distraught because she tried to have Sentinel One killed, Tina flew from the table and tried to get out of the house but couldn't open the front door.

Sentinel One approached her, pounding on the door, crying, "Stupid door won't open." He picked her head up, saying, "If it weren't for Alex, we wouldn't be married right now."

A shocked Tina asked, "Then you're not mad at me for lying about how Alex was after me and I needed somebody to protect me?"

"How can I be angry at someone as cute as you? But you are going to have to tell Alpha one. But don't worry, I'll be with you no matter what happens."

Sentinel One lay Tina on her stomach on the couch, took off her negligee, and gently massaged her entire body back and front.

During the body rub, Tina moaned softly, saying, "Don't even think of stopping. You have just the right touch that I need to help me relax."

After that, Tina stood and gave Sentinel One a long hug. He patted her bare tush, saying, "It's time you got dressed."

Once Tina was dressed, she sat on Sentinel One's shoulder as they walked to Alpha One's office.

13

The truth revealed

Tina nervously stared at the name on the dark wooden door, Alpha One, then slowly entered, holding onto her husband's hand. Sentinel One picked her up and stood her on a dark wooden chair so she could see who she was speaking to.

Sam, Alpha One, stared at the scared Sprite and asked, "What can I do for you, Little One."

Tina swallowed hard, then said, "Sam, Sir. Do you remember me saying that there may be a spy in the Omega Squadron?"

"Yes, I remember, and I still believe there is a spy among us."

"I know who that spy is. It is me. You see, I am not from a remote part of the Galaxy but from the swamps of Epsilon Prime. Alex found me, gave me a home, if you could call it that, and then hired me to be what he called Little Flee; in other words, I was the flea in the ointment. That meant I had to do what Mr. Alex told me whether I liked it or not, so I obeyed his every command without question. Do you remember Project Dragonfly? And how you wanted to establish an outpost outside Bristol, England, on Earth with plans to capture Alex, and it fell apart. Do you remember the project Sparrow to set up an operation in the Blue Ring System to capture Alex there? But it became a fiasco? I was to flee in your ointment at those places. I was the one who gave Alex a blow-by-blow of what was happening. I was Alex's mistress, which I hated, and I had to sleep with him when he wanted nooky and I had several miscarriages. I am tired of being Alex's puppet, and I don't like what Mr. Alex is doing to the Omega Squadron, so I'm turning myself in."

Sam stared at Tina and then stated, "Well, Little One, don't go anywhere because I want to ask you more questions later. I have never met a Sprite quite like you. They're always fun-loving and playing jokes. But if you're serious and are telling the truth, there's only one punishment for treason, and that is death."

A sorrowful Tina stared up at Sentinel One, jumped off the chair, walked out the door, and made her way to the Hot Springs.

Tina carefully walked around the bubbling mud pools to a shimmering Hot Spring. She smiled and said, "Hi, Ruthie. Would you mind if I joined you?"

Tina removed her clothes, slipped into the warm water, closed her eyes, and tried to relax.

Ruthie asked, "I know body language, and yours says something is bothering you. Do you want to unload your burden? I've got big shoulders."

After Tina had unloaded everything she had told Sam, Ruthie dressed and said, "I'll put a good word into Sam for you." Then she left.

Tina closed her eyes to try to relax when she heard steps approaching the hot spring. Without opening her eyes, she stated, "If you're here to try to convince me to go back to work for you, Mr. Alex, you've got another thing coming. Because the answer is no. I'm tired of all the hurt that I've helped you to do. I'm tired of sleeping with you, and I'm tired of the way you've been treating me. I'm a Sprite and should be playing games like Tree Dodging and Boulder Racing instead of being your secret henchman. I still have nightmares about how you talked me into setting Sentinel One up so you could kill him. Surprise, he is now my husband, thanks to you. Now leave before my husband finds out you're talking to me when I'm naked."

Alex knelt by Tina's back and stated, "You know I just can't let you go and risk you spilling the beans on everything I've done and the plans I have for the Mandroids."

"If you're gonna kill me, do it and save Sam the trouble of executing me for treason."

Alex placed his hands on Tina's shoulders and gently massaged her neck, working his way down her chest to put her off guard. Tina then gasped as Alex put his arm around her throat, held her down, and plunged the knife deep into her chest. He quickly glanced around to see if anybody saw him. Then, nonchalantly follow the path back to the Omega One Headquarters.

Alex was almost to his secret hideout when he stumbled upon Darrin approaching him, munching on a hamburger. Alex put on a smile and questioned, "Have you found a way to capture Ruthie and bring her to me? I'll double the price."

"Ruthie is a slippery eel, and It's gonna take some time for me to devise a plan to get her."

"You know where to find me if you change your mind,"

Darrin studied Alex's body language as he walked away. Then he stared up the path to the Hot Springs and muttered, "Oh Lord, no, he didn't." and ran up the path as fast as he could. When he saw Tina's lifeless body floating face up in the water with a knife in her chest. He hauled her out, wrapped his shirt around her, and screamed, "I need help! Tina's been stabbed!"

Darrin rushed into the doctor's office twelve minutes later with a bloody Tina in his arms, shouting, "I have an emergency. Help somebody,"

Doc Stevenson rushed into the office, saw Tina, and had Darrin put her on the exam table. Then she stated, "Scrub up because you're gonna help me save the life of a Sprite." She checked Tina's life signs and stated, "She's gone into cardiac arrest! Darrin, get me the Automatic External Defibrillator on the wall."

Some ten minutes later, a sorrowful Doc Stevenson said, "Call It."

Darrin looked at his watch and stated somberly, "It's 3:08 PM. I'll inform Sentinel One about the loss of his wife."

Just then, the heart monitor began to beep slowly. Doc Stevenson shouted, "Come on, Tina, you can do it; yes, that's it. Keep it up, girl. The Doc then shouted, Yes! She's back."

The next day, Tina opened her eyes and saw the doctor smiling at her, who said, "Welcome back, Little One. You gave us quite a scare. There's somebody here to see you."

Sentinel One entered the room, handed the dozen red roses to Tina, knelt by her bedside, and held her hand, smiling,

A surprised Tina asked, "Do you still love me even after you know the horrible truth and the things that I've done?"

"Of course, I still love you, my Sweet, my Little One. Outside of the joy Lord Jesus Christ puts in my life, you're my Sunshine, the one who puts a smile on my face every day. Oh, Sam has dropped all charges against you. Because he did some research and discovered the horrendous life you lived while working for Alex."

Tina sat up and tried to get out of bed, shouting, "Oh my gosh, Mandy is heading into a trap in Chicago; I gotta stop her!"

Sentinel One held Tina down, saying, "Settle down before the doctor puts you out,"

"You don't understand; I told Mr. Alex to set a trap and kill Mandy."

Sentinel One was able to get Tina to lay back down, saying, "Sam will inform Mandy of the situation,"

"You don't understand; as soon as Mandy gets in her rented car, it's gonna blow up."

Just then, Mandy walked into the room with a box of Frosty Nuts, gave them to Tina, and asked, "What's gonna explode?"

A shocked Tina asked, "What are you doing here when you're supposed to be on Earth dead?"

"The Retrieval pad is on the frits, so my trip to Earth will have to be postponed,"

Tina gave Mandy a long hug and then said, "I was Mr. Alex's Flee in the ointment, sort a speak, and he had me set a trap to kill you on Earth,"

Mandy stared at Tina for a few seconds, then said, "You are the spy?"

"Yes. Hey, if we act fast, we can catch Mr. Alex in his secret hideout. Get me my clothes, and I'll bring you there."

With Tina dressed, Sentinel One put her on his shoulder, and she directed him and Mandy to a huge mass of hanging vines in the jungle. The vines parted them to reveal an old stone house.

Sentinel One and Mandy searched the rooms lavishly decorated with expensive furniture from all over the Planetary Alliance. Mandy slowly pushed open a creaky door and almost passed out from the foul stench. She searched the room, which was laden with cobwebs and garbage. She pointed to a four-foot by four-foot rusty cage in one corner of the room, which had straw covering the floor.

Tina stated, "This is where Alex keeps me; those rags hanging on that piece of rope strung across the corner of the room were my clothes, and over in the other corner was my toilet."

A shocked Mandy inquired, "Why did you stay with that monster, Alex?"

"He told me the humans were out to beat me with a rubber hose if I didn't do what they said, so Mr. Alex hid me in here to protect me. But once in a while, I had to wear a fancy negligee and sleep with him because he wanted sex. But when Sentinel One took care of me in the cave, I realized Mr. Alex was lying to me. Then, when Sentinel One held me against his bare body to keep me warm that night, I felt someone loved me for the first time in my life. So I mated with him, and now Sentinel One is my husband, as you humans would say."

Mandy screamed in rage, "The next time I see Alex, so help me, I'm going to kill him where he stands!" Mandy contacted Sam on her computer watch, saying, "Tina just brought Sentinel One and me to Alex's hideout. But he fled before we arrived. I'd post a guard here just in case he comes back."

Sentinel One noticed blood on Tina's white blouse, peeked at her bandage, and said, "I need to get you home and change that bandage,"

In Sentinel One's home, he gently lay Tina on the couch, took off her blouse and bra, removed the bloody bandage, then, put on a new dressing, and asked, "For as long I can remember, we've been friends, and you always told me to keep our hugs and back rubs to PG13, which I had no problem doing. But when I had to take care of your wounds in the cave, you allowed me to see you naked for the first time. Then, in the morning, you wanted to get into it. Why the change?"

"Yes, we've been besties for a long time, and besties help each other in times of trouble. I figured that there was nothing wrong with you seeing me without my clothes on because you were helping me get better. You snuggled up to me all night, keeping me warm, gave me ideas, and I wanted to bless you for your help in the morning, so I gave you me."

But you are a Sprite,"

Tina stood on the couch and stated, "I am a thirty-five-inch tall, 29-year-old Sprite who knows what she wants, and that is you. So come here, Mate of mind, and give me some loving,"

A doubtful Sentinel One stared at Tina for a moment and said, "When you were working for Alex, you said that you were his mistress, meaning a prostitute. Do you really love me, or are you just performing the duties of a prostitute right now?"

With her head down, Tina stated, "I can understand why you would say something like that. I didn't tell you that I'm ashamed of what Alex did to me. I should have said that he raped me several times."

Sentinel One took a sobbing Tina in his arms and gave her a long hug when someone knocked on the front door. Tina covered herself as he opened it, saying, "Ruthie, you are just the one I wanted to see. Tina needs your help,"

"You want me to change her bandages and take care of her until she is better."

"You guessed it,"

"Good, I'll be here for the morning meal and stay until you get back."

Sentinel One kissed Tina and said, "I'll be back in a couple of hours, then we can pick up where we left off,"

"Promise?" asked Tina.

"I Promise,"

Tina then stated, "Stay away from Ariana because she's out to take you away from me."

"Don't worry, I will."

On Crater Lake Beach, Ariana approached Sentinel One clad in green hot pants and a halter top. Gave him a hug then asked, "You want to go for a walk along the beach? I know of a private place where we can sit, relax, and enjoy the sun?"

"My wife Tina would not appreciate us spending time together, and you know, as well as I do, that our clothes won't stay on for long when we are alone. What you have to say can be shared here amongst everybody on the beach."

Sentinel One held up his right index finger and said, "However, your offer is very tempting."

Just then, a long, loud, hideous howl filled the air, and a creature nearly the size of a horse, with long, bone-white, shaggy hair and massive golden eyes with three-inch long fangs, charged out of the jungle and onto the beach. Turned and charged them.

Ariana shouted, "It's a Snow Wolf! Everyone off the beach, Sentinel One, get behind me." She pointed her right hand towards the charging beast and let go of a blast of energy that only slowed the ferocious animal. Ariana let go of another blast of energy from her fingertips, which only infuriated the Snow Wolf.

The Omega Squadron rushed on the beach with their energy weapons firing, but it did not stop the beast from charging them.

Moe, also known as Beta, a five-foot-two-inch-tall woman with brown hair and eyes, limped forward, pointed her cane at the beast, and fired a blast of yellow energy at it to no avail.

Sentinel One glanced around and asked, "Where is the other Snow Wolf? Because they travel in pairs." He then slowly approached the raging animal with everybody screaming, "Stay back, get away from him, you're gonna get yourself killed."

When Sentinel One was a foot from the raging animal, it didn't seem to notice him. He turned to Tippy and stated, "Fire an electromagnetic charge at the Snow Wolf."

Tippy ordered, "Okay, everybody, set your weapons to electromagnetism and fire!"

As waves of an electromagnetic field surrounded the raging Snow Wolf, it vanished. Sentinel One stated, "It seems that whoever is after the androids is using solid holographic projections against us. However, we must treat them as real because we don't know when whoever it is will switch a holographic beast for a real one."

Sam walked up to Sentinel One and stated, "You took a big risk by approaching that Snow Wolf unarmed. Of course, you know the other snow wolf could have been in the jungle."

14

Broken ties

Late that afternoon, Sentinel One was in the cafeteria with Mandy, talking to Darrin, when they heard the howl of a cat. They rushed out the front door, and there was Ruthy, dressed in jeans and a black T-shirt, facing down a huge Jaguar, saying, "You're gonna get yours for ruining my quiet time. So give me your best, you overgrown house cat."

The Jaguar leaped towards Ruthie; she flipped to her right and kicked the cat in its side as it passed. The big cat let go a yelp, quickly turned, and swiped at her left side, ripping it open. Ruthie grabbed a hanging vine from a nearby tree, jumped on the Jaguar's back, slipped the vine around the cat's neck, and pulled it tight until it fell on its side, out cold. Tippy, Debbie, and Moe rushed to the scene and put the big cat in a cage before it came too.

Sentinel One looked to his left and saw Kimmy looking dejected and for lawn sitting under a tree not too far away. Approached and sat on her left and questioned, "Why the long face?"

"Yesterday, I put on a pretty orange gingham dress, wore Greg's favorite perfume, and tried to be romantic with him. He ignored me, so I gave him a tender kiss on his cheek. Instead of a passionate response, he screamed, "Get away from me, you miserable bucket of bolts. He then landed a hard right cross to my face, sending me to the ground, but before I could get up, he kicked me in my side and stormed off. I found out earlier this morning that Greg had Tippy send him back to Earth. I may be an Android Humanoid, but I have feelings as strange as it may seem." Kimmy stared at Sentinel One and asked, "What do you do when you feel empty, and your world has just crashed around you?"

Sentinel One gave Kimmy a hug and said, "When everything you've known seems to have vanished, turn to Christ, and he will fill you with his love."

"But I'm just a bucket of bolts, a conglomerate of wires and circuits. How can the Almighty love that?"

"The scripture says whoever will come let him come drink of the waters freely. You are a whoever, so the Lord's arms are big enough to love you,"

Just then, Tina landed in front of Sentinel One and asked, "What's been happening with you, bestie?"

"I thought we'd cuddle this afternoon after some personal time."

Tina quickly snapped back, "Sprites don't interact with humans."

"We are married, and what about the time you wanted to get into it when we were in the cave?

"That must've been your imagination because Sprites and humans do not interact with each other sexually. We're energized and sparkly and only interact with other Sprites. I just came by to tell you I'll be living in the Sprite community across Crater Lake."

A confused Sentinel One stated, "But we are husband and wife according to spite law."

"You must have me mixed up with some other Sprites because we are just besties. I'll see you later, Sentinel One," and flew away.

Sentinel One stared at Kimmy and said, "That I did not expect. Maybe she'll recant and come back."

Kimmy smiled sheepishly and stated, "Sprite Kayli, had a long talk with Tina the other day about how she is a slap in the face to the Sprite community by claiming you as her mate. Tina looked at Sprite Kayli, paused momentarily, and then apologized for marrying a human. Sprite Kayli questioned, "Have you gone before a human pastor and have it in writing?" Tina shook her head. No, they were going to do it in a day or two. Kayli then stated, "Then you are not mated to that human. Leave him, repent of your wrongdoing, and live in the Sprite community.

Doc Stevenson then erased Tina's memory of her being on the Omega Squadron for security reasons."

Sentinel One stated, "We do have a marriage certificate, but I guess it's not worth the paper it's written on. You want to take a walk on the beach?"

Kimmy stood, took Sentinel One by his hand, and lifted him, saying, "I would love nothing better than to walk on the beach with you."

On a quiet section of the white sandy beach, Kimmy stared into Sentinel One's eyes, and the pressure of kissing him rose inside her. But she resisted, thinking, *"I'm just a bucket of bolts, and I'll probably be rejected."*

Sentinel One took Kimmy in his arms and gave her a long, passionate kiss on her lips. Kimmy's eyes widened with a surprised look, and she responded passionately. The two of them fell on the white sand together, kissing.

Somewhere around an hour later, Kimmy sat up, fixed her blouse and bra, and said, "I think we should stop before we can't, and I displease the Lord greatly by going all the way with you."

"I have never met a woman as passionate as you."

"But I'm just a conglomerate of wires and mechanisms that resembles a human female."

Doc Stevenson walked up, stared at the two full of sand, smiled, and said, "I see the two of you found each other."

Sentinel One asked, "I know you didn't come all this way just to engage in minor chitchat. What's the bad news?"

Doc Stevenson sat on the white sand next to Kimmy and said, "I am so sorry for misdiagnosing you. You don't have a mechanical brain. You have a real brain with a cap on top of it resembling a human brain."

"In English doc," stated Kimmy.

"You are a hybrid Mandroid; when they put your brain inside your skull, they put a brain-like cap on top of it. That brain-like cap sends signals directly to the different parts of your body to keep it functioning."

A shocked Kimmy stated, "Then I'm not just a bucket of bolts but a real person that has a soul and a spirit encased in a mechanical body. YES!"

Doc Stevenson said, "I am so sorry for destroying your marriage with Greg."

"Don't be, because all things work together for the good who love God to them who are called according to his purpose. By Greg walking away from me, I met the man of my dreams, Sentinel One; thank you, Doc."

"Then I'll leave you 2 to continue what you were doing."

Kimmy stared at Sentinel One, smiled, and said, "Come here, Stud Muffin, you're mine,"

Hours later, Kimmy ran into the jungle to be alone. Sentinel One found her on her knees crying, knelt on her right side, and asked, "Are you alright?"

Because of what we just did, I was convicted and knew I had sinned greatly against the Lord and had to be alone with my Saviour. Please forgive me for forcing you to get into it with me."

"This means we have to get into the Word of God more and pray to maintain our walk with Christ so we can stay out of the flesh."

Kimmy stated, "Yes, we need to do that, but our walk with our Saviour isn't the dos and don'ts, but it's what he did on the Cross. It's by Christ and the Cross that we stand and go forward. It's what Christ did for us when we gave our lives to Him, and we continue through the Cross. If we try in our own strengths with all types of religious activities, it's dead works."

A grateful Sentinel once stated, "Thank you for correcting me. However, there's something about you that completes me, and I have this feeling that we should be together."

Kimmy threw her arms around Sentinel One, Saying, "I was so scared that you were going to leave me after what we did."

Sentinel One helped Kimmy to her feet, saying, "This may be my flesh speaking, but sex with you was great.".

Kimmy giggled, saying, "Yes, it was, but let's not do it again until after our wedding."

Alex walked up to them in the jungle, smiled politely, and asked, "Kimmy, why do you hang around this useless piece of garbage resembling a human?"

Kimmy winked at Sentinel One, turned to Alex, and said, "I guess I wasn't thinking straight. But thanks for reminding me how wrong I was." Kimmy slowly put her arms around Alex's neck, gave him a long kiss on his lips, then asked, "What do you say we waste this sorry piece of human flesh, Sentinel One?" Then, she took the energy pistol from Alex's side and said sweetly, "Could you please let me waste Sentinel One right here right now in the jungle where no one will know what happened to him,"

Alex smiled and said, "Sure, be my guest. Then I'll let you play around with the Mandroids I have hidden in the basement of my secret hideout."

Kimmy pointed the energy pistol at Sentinel One, chuckled sinisterly, and said, "It's time to die." Quickly spun around and fired a blast of energy at Alex, sending him to the ground out cold.

A shocked Sentinel One asked, "What did you do that for? We could have got him to tell us who Mister Big is."

"I didn't kill him."

"Are you sure you didn't kill him?".

"Remind me to tell you the story, a night with a Madman. But right now, we have some Mandroids to free."

In a well-lit basement of Alex's secret hideout, Sentinel One and Kimmy stared at four wooden crates stacked in a corner. Sentinel One opened the top one and saw the head and body of a woman with messy light brown hair. Then said, "I found the Mandroids. This one looks like she should be in her mid-thirties by the looks of it. Call Tippy and inform her that we found the missing Mandroids."

"I did and can't get through. He must have a dampening field around the building to prevent them from calling for help. We're gonna have to assemble them ourselves."

Sentinel One lay all the body parts of the one in the box on the floor, then began to assemble her, saying, "This one sure has a big butt. Hey, can you find some clothes so they're not running around naked?"

An hour and a half later, all the Mandroids were put together and dressed, but Sentinel One could not figure out how to turn them on no matter how hard he pressed their upper left breast.

Kimmy approached the woman with brown hair, got up to her face, and hollered, "You are all together and assembled, but we're having a problem turning you back on. Is there any way you can help us?"

The Mandroid shook violently for two minutes, then stopped; she opened her brown eyes, stared at Sentinel One, and stated, "I do not have a big tushy, and did you have to handle my boobs when you were putting on my arms?"

"A simple thank you would be nice,"

"Oh, by the way, I'm Alice Birdson, and thank you for rescuing me from my torment."

Sentinel One asked, "Can you help us turn the others on?"

Some twenty-nine minutes later, all the Mandroids were turned on, and Kimmy asked, "Just who are you guys?"

"I'm Jeff Stearns, that's Tom Marks on my right; next to him are Terrie Joan Ramsey and Alice Birdson, and we are the sole survivors of the city of Odessa that was destroyed just over1000 years ago."

Jeff approached Kimmy and gently brushed his hand against her face, saying, "A hybrid Mandroid, nice. Maybe you and I can get together this evening and get to know one another."

Kimmy held Sentinel One's arm, saying, "Sorry, this is my hubby-to-be."

Sentinel One asked, "Do you know what secret project Alex had you guys designed for besides imitating a wooden box?"

"Don't be a smart mouth. All any of us know is that we were going to be shipped to Chicago, Illinois," stated Alice.

Sentinel One stated, "Let's get you guys back to Omega One Headquarters to be debriefed."

While walking back, Alice snuggled up to Sentinel One and whispered, "How about you and I find a quiet spot later and make some pleasurable memories."

Kimmy nudged her, saying, "He's spoken for, Tramp."

"Give me five minutes with him, and he'll change his mind in a heartbeat."

Kimmy grinned from ear to ear, saying, "You're on. If Sentinel One doesn't warm up to you in five minutes, you serve me and Sentinel One our morning meal for a month. But if you're right, I'll be your slave for a month and he is yours."

Late that evening, a stunned Alice walked out of the beautiful garden and stared at Kimmy, saying, "The guy is a robot, an automaton; he's not human. I did everything I could to seduce Sentinel One, and he ignored me."

"I'll see you at Sentinel One's home so you can cook our morning meal and don't be late."

Alice asked, "What did you do to him to prevent him from looking at another woman?"

"It's called love and commitment. Study it, and you will learn something.

In Sam's office three hours later, he sat behind his mahogany desk. Stared at Sentinel One, Alice, Kimmy, and Terry then stated, "The three of you are gonna be going to Chicago, Illinois, on Earth; you will meet your contact who will tell you where you're going to be staying and what the plan is concerning Mr. Big. Kimmy, I'm sorry but I'm going to be sending you to the Blue Ring System because there's a bunch of Androids there that are barely staying alive because all that has come against them. Your job will be to get them to the safety of Planet HP5. It's gonna take you quite a while, so be prepared for a long stay. You are suitable for the job because of who you are and what you are. I am sorry I have to split up you and Sentinel One, but this mission has to come before your relationship."

Tippy brought Sentinel One and the two women to a ten-foot by ten-foot white room and stated, This is the new transporter room."

"How can that be when It's just a white room,"

Tippy typed in the computer, Little Branch Cafe Coffee shop1251 South Prairie Chicago Illinois, Earth.

The white room instantly transformed into a quaint cafe with tree stumps for stools at the counter. Tippy stated, "Walk in and sit at the bar, and I'll transport you to that spot. It's the newest thing in transporters, a virtual room where you see where you're going."

Sentinel One stated, "You're going to send that poor little coffee shop into a panic when they see three people instantly appear on barstools."

"Oh, yeah, I forgot about Earth being technologically backward. OK, go into the restrooms, wait for about a minute, and then walk out, and you will be there; however, nobody will see you appear.

Sitting at the counter in the Little Branch Café, Sentinel One, Alice and Terrie ordered coffee.

Terrie questioned, "So, now what do we do?"

A Three-foot tall woman sat next to Sentinel One and said, "You will be living in an apartment building on South King Drive. Alice and Terrie will be staying with me and Ruthie in the next apartment."

"Tina!" shouted Sentinel One and she gave him a kiss.

She smiled, saying, "Alice, Terrie, you two stay here; I need to talk to Sentinel One,"

Outside, Sentinel One put Tina on his shoulders and asked, "I thought you didn't Remember me."

"It seems the procedure to remove certain parts of a person's memory doesn't work on Sprites. I have to apologize to you for being deceptive. I was desperate to get away from Mr. Alex, so when he told me to set you up so he could kill you, I saw an opportunity to manipulate you into being my protector when I was shot and fell into that pickery Bush. That's why I didn't mind sleeping with you naked and got into it with you in the morning. I lied to Kayli and told her that we didn't go before a pastor and didn't have a marriage certificate because she was pressuring me so much. Will you forgive me, hubby of mine?"

"Sure,"

Just then, Sentinel One received a phone call on his watch and answered, "Kimmy, how are you doing?"

"I'm good, but I'm gonna have to break off our relationship because the Lord has shown me that I've been running after everything in pants, and I can't do that anymore if I'm gonna walk with Him."

"I understand walking with your Saviour is more important than a relationship with someone. Lord bless you and keep you safe on your mission. Goodbye"

Tina asked, "You and Kimmy got together?"

"We got carried away in the jungle one day and wanted to be together, but as you heard, it didn't work out." Sentinel One put Tina on the ground in front of him. He got on his knees and asked, "Are you still ashamed to be married to me because the spike community frowns on it?"

Tina threw her arms around Sentinel One's neck and cried, "Please take me back."

"I never divorced you as my wife; besides, Kimmy can't fit into your clothes. Just kidding." Sentinel One gave Tina a long, passionate kiss on her lips.

A woman who was passing by stopped and stated, "How dare you molest that poor little child,"

Tina faced the middle-aged woman, stuck out her chest, saying, "Seriously, lady? Does a 12-year-old child have boobs as big as mine?" And no, my boobs are not falsies. They're real, and if you don't believe me, come into the women's room, and I'll show you. Ohh, I'm 29 years old, and this man is my husband."

In the hotel room, Ruthie stated, "The head of this organization is Alex who wants 6 Mandroids so he can put the brains of a group called the Sinister six into their bodies. Which means Patsy and her Mandroid friends are gonna die. Alice, I need you to come with me."

On the top floor of a tall glass office building, Ruthie marched into an office, got in the secretary's face, and said, "Tell Alex that Ruthie is here to see him about his toy box."

Ruthie then barged in the door to her right and up to the man behind the desk dressed in a business suit, saying, "You want six Mandroids? I've got them. Oh, and Mr. Roach isn't going to be calling you because I got rid of him, I think."

Alex leaned forward and asked, "Just how do you know about my toy box?"

"While Mr. Alex was getting me ready to put my brain in a Mandroid, he told me about how your six henchmen are in serious trouble with the law, and you're trying to hide them by putting them in Mandroids."

"Can you do better?"

Alice entered the office, and Ruthie stated, "This is Alice, and she is willing to let you have her Mandroid body because she is dying of brain cancer."

Alex stood, walked up to Alice, opened her blouse, lifted her bra, and squeezed her firm breast. He then pulled her slacks and underwear down and intently examined her pelvic area with his hands. He then sat behind his desk as an embarrassed Alice made herself decent and stated, "If the other three women and two men are as well put together as this one, you've got yourself a deal."

Ruthie inquired, "Before I take payment, I want to see the Sinister 6, so I know I am not dooming six people to death because of a scam."

Just then, four women and two men walked out from a room behind Ruthie, and Alex stated, "Here's your proof: my six henchmen are ready to claim their new android bodies."

Ruthie then stated, "I would like you to meet the OSF."

Tippy burst into the room with Moe, Debbie, and the rest of the team, as Ruthie hollered, "I got it all on tape; arrest them." Alex sat in is chair, pushed a button on his desk. The floor opened under the chair sending Alex down and escaped.

Back at the OSF, Sam called Victor into his office. A short, well-built man with dark brown hair in his mid-thirties clad in jeans and a green t-shirt entered and Sam stated, "Victor, I'm the Galaxy Sentinel's right-hand man. I also run an organization called the Agency, from which the Mysterious Strangers have their headquarters, and the OSF. At my age, I'm getting too old to burn the candle at both ends, so Victor, as of right now, you are Omega One who will be in charge of the OSF." Sam then spun around and walked out the door.

Victor called in Sprite Kayli and asked, "Who gave you the authority to tell sprites that they can't marry a human? Because of you, Sentinel One and Tina almost broke up. And I don't know how many other Sprite relationships you threw a monkey wrench in the works. From here on in, if I hear you telling another Sprite that they can't marry or have a relationship with a human, you're gonna be looking for a new job. Do I make myself clear? Oh, and tell Darrin I want to see him."

As soon as Darrin walked into the office, Victor lit into him, saying, "I'm sending you back to Earth because that's where you belong, not on this complex flirting with everything that wears a skirt. Don't worry about Misty. King Mix has already made plans to take care of her and the little one. Now get out of my office." He made his way down to Crater Lake beach and sat on a blanket next to Tina, who was wearing a blue micro bikini and asked, "Are you feeling a little Darren today?"

"Sentinel One and I renewed our relationship last night. He is busy building the back porch, and I'm getting it tanned to look good for him. And yes, Darrin got fresh with me.

"I sent him back to Earth. Oh, I'm now Omega One in charge of the OSF. I want you and Sentinel one take care of things for a short while. I'm going to Earth for a short vacation. See you when I get back."

15

The mysterious woman

Victor boarded the sky tram in Rutland, Vermont. Greeted a cute, slender five-foot-five Asian woman in her late twenties with short black hair who silently grinned at Victor as she sat in the sky tram with him.

Victor commented as the sky tram began its downward trip, "I must say your light blue slot suit looks great on you. Hey, will you look at those beautiful mountains on your left?"

The woman quietly smiled and looked at what Victor was pointing at.

Somewhere halfway down the sky tram ride, it stopped. Victor quickly looked around, wondering what had happened, and then he figured more people were getting on. He gazed at the woman and asked, "Where are you from?" But she looked at him, smiled sweetly, and remained silent. Victor looked at his watch and muttered, "I wonder what's wrong because it's been over an hour we've been sitting here." He gently patted the woman's left shoulder, saying, "We'll be alright." The woman shifted her seating position and screamed as she fell off the sky tram. Victor studied the woman lying motionless on the grass below, glanced around, climbed up, shimmied along the cable to the nearest tower, and then climbed down.

On the ground, he looked up and said, "Whoa, I never thought I could do that." Then he rushed to the woman and checked to see if she was still alive.

In a soft voice, the woman stated, "I'm Susan Wong from Rockland, Vermont, and I don't believe I was that clumsy to fall off the tram."

"Do you hurt anywhere?"

"No, but would you mind if I lie here for a while."

"Sure, no problem. Would you mind if I poke around your body to see if you broke anything? Trust me, I'm not trying to get fresh."

Susan giggled as Victor pushed and rubbed Susan's legs, arms, pelvic area, and chest, then stated, "You're going to be a little sore for a while, but outside of that, you're a lucky woman."

Susan put her head in Victor's lap and said, "Thank you for risking your life to come to me on the ground."

"I couldn't let you lie there all alone."

But Susan didn't answer and figured she fell asleep.

Victor carried Susan to the tram tower, sat her on the grass, and leaned her back against the tower. Then he sat on her left, put his arm around her waist, and drifted off to sleep.

The next morning, Susan woke, stretched, and said, "I feel like I've slept on a bed of rocks." She put her right hand in her pocket, pulled out two granola bars, gave one to Vic, and said, "The morning meal is served."

After that, Susan stood, did some warming-up exercises, and stared at Victor, saying, "Take off that t-shirt." Susan stepped behind him, put her hands on his shoulders, and gave him a good back rub. Then she pointed to the woods, saying, "We go that way to the road."

"But the tram platform is down this mountain, which shouldn't be a problem."

"True, but when they find out we spent the night on the tram, we will be surrounded by newspaper reporters, people taking pictures, and police asking questions, which is something I want to avoid because I hate crowds. So we go this way through the woods."

On a wooded country road, Victor said, "I need to get my car."

"Okay, you get your car. I'll be sitting on this rock waiting for you to bring me to my hotel, and like I said, I dislike lots of people."

At the Holladay Inn, Victor was about to say goodbye to Susan when she asked him if he would come to her room for a cup of coffee.

In Susan's room on the third floor, she kicked off her shoes, took off her blazer, and loosened her blouse, saying, "Be out in a jiffy; I gotta wash several layers of crud off my body."

Later, Susan walked out of the bathroom in a white fuzzy robe, made a pot of coffee, and gave Victor a mug. She sat in front of him and asked, "How would you like to be my bodyguard? I pay good, plus plenty of fringe benefits. No, showering and sleeping with me is not one of the fringe benefits."

"Let me think about that,"

Just then, someone knocked on the door. Susan opened it, and a tall man in his forties pushed Susan to the floor and kicked her side. Victor sprang to his feet, grabbed the man by his shirt, and landed a hard right cross to his face, sending him stumbling backward. When the man charged Victor again, he landed 3 Roundhouse kicks to the his face, sending him stumbling out the door. Victor helped a shaken Susan to her feet, put his hand on her bare right side, and asked, "Does it hurt where I am pushing?"

"No, I'm alright.' She gently put her hand on Victor's, saying with a smile, "Being a little frisky, or is this your way of getting me in bed with you?"

Victor smiled sheepishly and quickly removed his hand and apologized.

Susan giggled and said, "Relax. I was just teasing you. Why don't you take a shower? That way, I can get dressed without exposing myself to you even more."

Victor glanced at Susan, closed her robe, put his arms around her, and kissed her lips. Susan put her arms around Victor, kissed him, and said, "I was wondering how long it was going to take before you kissed me. Now take your shower so I can put some clothes on."

Victor let go of Susan and said, "You've fallen and have been bumped multiple times, but yet, there are no bruises on your body. Normally, any woman your age getting that beat up would have blackened blue marks all over her body, but you don't. I know this because I peeked when that guy pushed you to the floor, causing your bathrobe to fly open."

"What can I say? I'm a resilient Little Bugger. Now take your shower. Then you can put your underwear and pants on, and I'll give you a good back rub."

The next morning, Victor woke at six, dressed, opened the door connecting the two rooms, and woke Susan. She moaned, "Is it that time already?" and staggered to the bathroom in her powder blue baby doll PJs to wash up.

Afterward, she opened the bathroom door and promptly collapsed on the floor. Victor picked her up and carried her to the bed; she opened her left eye and smiled, saying, Good morning, my Sweet."

"Please get dressed so we can get to the fun park before it's mobbed with people."

Susan stood, put her arms around Victor, kissed his lips, and softly said, "Please be patient with me." She rested her head on his shoulder, closed her eyes, and asked, "Can we stay like this for a while?"

Victor put his face against Susan's cheek and asked, "You're trembling. What's wrong?"

"I can't tell you right now."

While Victor watched, Susan went on the mammoth slide six times at the fun park. After, she rushed to him and said, "Don't be such a party pooper; loosen up and have some fun."

"I'm here to make sure no one attacks you. Now sit and tell me about the nightmare you had last night."

Susan sat on Victor's right, took a sip of her lemonade, and said, "Alright, this is what happened. One afternoon, I lay in a grassy field looking up at the fluffy clouds and fell asleep. When I came too, some guy was raping me. I was so horrified and was about to scream when he belted me and knocked me out. I came too sometime later, fixed myself, and tried to forget the ordeal."

"So you got into a lot of fun and excitement to drown out the memory of what happened."

"Pretty much,"

"Shall we go to a quiet park?"

"Yes, we shall." Stated Susan, eager to be alone with Victor.

In a wooded area of the park, Victor loosens Susan's blouse and gently rubs her shoulders, helping her to relax and let go of the emotional hurt because of the rape.

Susan sighed contentedly as Victor massaged her shoulders, which was soothing and comforting. Then she said, "This feels wonderful, Victor. Thank you for taking care of my needs."

Victor slid his hands up under her blouse and gently rubbed her back down to her hips. Susan exhaled peacefully as Victor continued to work out the tension in her body and said, "Victor, you have such skilled hands. Your touch makes everything feel better. Thank you."

"Shall we sit under a tree and relax?"

"Sounds like a great idea," stated Susan.

They moved to a huge shade tree and found a comfortable spot. Susan rested her head against Victor's shoulder. She breathed in the calming fragrances and felt the warmth of Victor's embrace, saying, "This moment is pure perfection."

Over an hour later, Susan sat up and looked at Victor, who was sleeping on his back. She lay on his left side and kissed his lips, waking him. Then she said, "Thank you for helping me forget my past. Now stop being such a prude, and let's go back to the hotel,"

At the Holladay Inn, Susan stated, "Go in the bathroom, take everything off, wrap a bath towel around your waist, then lie on your stomach on the bed."

A few minutes later, Susan gazed at Victor on the bed with a towel covering his bottom for a bit, then proceeded to give him a complete body rub down.

Some two hours later, Victor woke, took off the towel, sat up, and said, "Thank you, Susan, for that complete body rub."

"Ah, please cover yourself."

"Why? We're good friends,"

The next morning, Victor sat on the edge of the bed and entered Susan's room through the connecting door in his brief. He saw her sleeping, got on his knees at the side of the bed, and cried, "I stand in your throne room, heavenly father, because of Christ and the cross in my life. Give Susan the strength to trust you." Victor then put on some Christian music and worshiped the Lord to keep his mind on his Saviour.

Susan woke, saw Victor in his underwear, and blushed, saying, "Shouldn't you put something more on besides those cute BVDs?"

"We've been together for over a month, and I believe it's alright for us to see each other in our underwear."

Susan sat on the edge of the bed in her pale blue step-ins, covered her chest with a pillow, and glared at Victor as she made her way to the bathroom to dress.

Sitting at a table in the Holladay Inn's dining room later that morning, Susan stated, "We need to respect each other's boundaries,"

"Say what?" questioned Victor.

"Ah, we need to be careful how we are dressed in front of each other,"

"Why? What was important was covered this morning, so I believe there is nothing wrong with seeing each other in our underwear because we're very close friends. Besides, you're the one who started it yesterday by giving me a body rub, so I figured you seeing me in my underwear was all right."

"That's it, I'm outta here," Susan sprang to her feet and stormed off.

Victor caught up to her in the lobby and said, "Susan, my Sweet, do you know you put your slacks on inside out and forgot to put on your bra?"

Susan glanced down at herself and then at Victor, then ran back to the room.

Victor entered Susan's room two minutes later as she was putting on her blouse. He wrapped his arms around her, enfolding her in a warm embrace.

Susan smiled, saying, "A big hug is just what I need right now. Your support means everything to me, and I cherish our relationship."

"I do love you, my Sweet, and you look cute in your underwear."

Susan smiled, saying, "Together, we'll face whatever life throws our way, standing strong in faith and devotion. Our bond is a precious gift from our Saviour, one that brings light and happiness into our lives. And with that, let's continue to nurture this love and cultivate its growth in our lives. With Christ with us, we will build a firm foundation filled with trust, tenderness, and mutual respect, serving as the bedrock of our enduring relationship."

Victor held up her bra and asked, "Forget something again?"

"Dang!" stated Susan, snatched her bra out of Victor's hand, went into the bathroom, coming out 5 minutes later, and asked, "Now am I presentable?"

Victor sat on the bed with Susan, held her hand, and asked, "What have you out of sorts today?"

"Last night is what did it. I'm used to being treated like a commodity, but you treated me with respect and love. Our time together last night blew me away. Please, please don't leave me like everybody else has."

"You're stuck with me whether you like it or not. Now, let's eat our morning meal."

Back in the dining room, Victor went to get Susan a plate of food. A heavy-set man clad in a tan plaid shirt who worked at the Institute, sat at Susan's table and said to her, "There you are, Kayli Aubrette. Do you know we've been looking all over creation for you?"

"I'm not going back, and that's final."

"The doctors have to correct the mistake, so come back to the hospital."

"Albert," moaned Kayli, "Why don't you take a powder."

"Stop giving me a hard time, and come back to the hospital so the doctors can fix the problem,"

"Why should I go back? So they can botch things up even worse? No, I won't."

"The doctors want to rectify the mess they made and give the Mandroid body to the one it was meant for."

"Why should I go back? So they can put my brain in the body of a jackass? No, I won't go back. Besides, they've probably already cremated my poor little body."

Albert questioned, "That man that is getting you a plate of food. Is he just someone helping you with your morning meal?"

"He's more than a friend. He is my lover and hopeful mate."

A shocked Albert questioned, "Tell me you didn't mix it up in bed with him,"

"You better believe I did, and we'll do it a lot more after we're mated. Why don't you take a walk off a short pier and stop bugging me?"

"You're gonna mate with a human? That will be the stupidest thing you've ever done, and you've pulled some boners in the past. What if he finds out who you really are?"

"Finds out what, that I'm a woman who has passions and desires that need to be fulfilled by a man."

"You know very well what I mean, Kayli."

Victor set a plate of food in front of Susan as Albert walked away and asked, "Who was that? A new friend?"

"No, just a pain in my sit-down." Susan gave Victor a peck on his right cheek, saying, "Be right back; nature is beckoning me."

"Huh?"

"Gotta use the potty,"

Some fifteen minutes later, Victor glanced at his watch, wondering where Susan was, and heard a commotion coming from the lobby. He sprang to his feet and ran into the lobby to see two men dragging Susan out the door into a gray Chevy. A young man gave Victor his motorcycle, saying, "Here, use this. Go after her,"

16

Feeling Betrayed

Victor followed the kidnapper's car until it came to a red light. Pulled alongside it, drove his fist through the side window, and hauled the man holding Susan through it. Put Susan on his motorcycle and drove off.

Susan glanced back, saying, "Don't look now, but they're following us, so step on it."

Victor weaved in and out of traffic at top speed, then through an open field. The car tried to give chase but was bogged down in the soft dirt.

On a small country road, Victor stopped the motorcycle, gave Susan a kiss, and then asked, "Who were those men?"

"I don't know, but I am truly grateful to have you in my life right now. So can we sit here and enjoy this beautiful moment of victory and take in nature that is all around us."

Victor sat on the stonewall on Susan's right and held her in his arms, saying, "You're gonna be alright."

Susan stated, sobbing, "I was scared something fears that they were gonna abuse me."

Victor reassured Susan by saying, "No one dare abuse you as long as I am around." He stood behind Susan, massaged her shoulders through her white blouse, and asked, "Just who are you?"

"What do you mean, who am I? I'm me, Susan Wong, the love of your life, your mate."

"There is something about you that sets you apart from all other women. I can't put my finger on it right now because of everything that's been happening. This may sound crazy, but you act as if you are from another planet."

Susan smiled sheepishly, then said, "Hey, how about that? I'm your spaced-out mate. Take me to your leader." Susan then giggled.

Back at the hotel, Victor gave the motorcycle back to the young man, checked out, and was getting in his car when Susan heard a woman holler, "Kayli Aubrette, wait up!"

She quickly ducked into the car, saying, "Let's get outta here fast so I can put this bad memory behind me."

On I-90 West somewhere in Ohio, Victor pulled his car to the side of the road, turned to Susan, and asked, "Are you feeling alright?"

A joyful Susan shouted, "We need to find a motel for the night because there is something I have to tell you but not here in the car."

"Can we wait, my Sweet for the motel because it's only four in the afternoon?"

In a motel later that day, Susan sat on the edge of the bed in a pair of red hot pants and a pink halter top. Showed a weak smile then stated, "I want to tell you this before we were mates. But after I tell you, you will probably walk out on me. You see, my real name is Kayli Aubrette, and I was a feisty 25-year-old, twenty-eight-inch tall Sprite from the Planet Pylee and was on security at the OSF when I had an accident that put me in the hospital. There was some mix-up, and my brain was put in a robot called a Mandroid. All the organs in my body, from my lungs, my heart, my stomach, intestines, everything is artificial. The heart pumps real blood, and the lungs pump real oxygen to keep the brain alive."

"An interesting story, Susan, but to me, you look, feel, and act like a real woman." Victor placed his hand on Susan's right leg, felt her soft, warm skin as he stroked it, and then said, "Susan, the softness of your body tells me that you are a human, not a robot. But the horror you're going through right now is beyond description, so I'll be with you to help you through this."

A shocked Susan asked, "You mean you're not gonna walk out on me."

"Why should I? You say you have an artificial body, but your brain is intact and is who you are. Hey, when I get old and Gray and wrinkly, I'll still have you, who will still be young and perky. Now, let's cuddle."

The next morning, in a nearby diner, Victor inquired, "Do you want to continue going west, or do you want to go back to the motel?"

That afternoon in the motel, Victor gently placed his hands on Susan's bare back and applied firm pressure as he kneaded her knots away. His movements were slow and deliberate, focusing entirely on her comfort. He then asked, "How does that feel?"

"It feels great, so don't stop."

As Victor continued working Susan's bare back, she glanced up at him, and he saw the warmth in her eyes. He smiles, knowing that he's making a difference in her life. Victor stated, "Sweet, you deserve to be pampered and cared for, so relax."

"Thank you, my Love."

"Anytime, my Sweet," stated Victor as his hands glided smoothly across Susan's soft, warm back, each movement flowing seamlessly into the next. He listens intently to the quiet sighs escaping her lips, relishing the knowledge that he's bringing her relief and pleasure. Victor's touch became even more sensitive, tracing the muscles of her body with the utmost care and dedication.

Susan stated, "That feels so good. Keep going,"

Absolutely," Victor said with renewed energy. He delicately worked his way down her spine, applying just the right amount of pressure to release the tension. Each stroke left Susan visibly relaxed as the knots melted away, leaving her feeling rejuvenated and restored.

A much relaxed Susan sat up in her powder blue panties, covering her chest with her hands, saying, "Thank you,"

"You're welcome," stated Victor with a smile. He paused momentarily, letting the silence envelop the air with a sense of tranquility.

As Susan lay down, Victor covered her with a blanket and questions, "Shall I call you Susan or Kayli?"

"I am Miss Susan Wong. Sprite Kayli Aubrette died in the hospital when they put her brain in this body."

"Who was that man you were talking to yesterday in the hotel?"

"That was Albert, who wants to be in charge of the Omega Strike Force and is trying to bring me back to the hospital. Where they will most likely put my brain in a jar, then give this Mandroid body to someone else. I say this is mine, and they can't have it. The Bible says all things work together for good to those who love God and those who are called according to his purpose. The Lord caused the doctors to be confused so my brain could be put in this body so I could be with you."

Later, Victor studied Susan's every movement as he watched her dress, remembering how soft and warm her body felt when he gave her a back rub. He then wondered, "How can Susan be a robot when everything about her says she's human? I think there is something wrong with her story. She's either covering something up, or she is delusional. Because no robot can feel soft and warm the way Susan's body does."

Victor then stated as a much relaxed Susan lay on the bed, "I'm going to the lobby for a cup of coffee. Be back later,"

As Victor was enjoying his hot Hazelnut coffee in the lobby, a tall gentleman in a blue business suit approached him. Showed him a picture of Susan and asked,

"Have you seen this woman Kayli Aubrette?"

A hesitant Victor stated, "Ah, no, what has she done?"

"She escaped from the hospital Sycho ward, saying she is a Pixie in a robot body. She goes into detail about how her robot body works and why she is trapped inside it."

"Is she violent?" questioned a curious Victor.

"No, but there's no telling what she's capable of doing when she's in that delusional state. I mean, she may think she has wings and jump off a building and kill herself."

Victor took the man's business card and put it in his shirt pocket, saying, "If I see this woman, I will call you." Then watched the man walk away and took a swallow of his coffee, thinking, *"Susan did say that the hospital was after her. Those men that kidnapped her looked like doctors, and how can a robot feel soft and warm?"*

Albert then sat in front of Victor, took a swallow of his black coffee, and stated, "You're the one who has been helping feisty Kayli Aubrette. Tell me where she is so I can bring her back to the hospital."

"I know of a Susan Wong but not a Kayli Aubrette. Hey, wait a minute. I did hear about her. Is she the one who died in a hospital because of a doctor's snafu?"

"Well, you see, she didn't actually die. The doctor made a mistake when they operated on her, and I'm here to bring her back so he can straighten things out."

"Don't you mean so they can make a bigger mess than the one they already made?"

"The doctors are not a bunch of stumblebums trying to do things in the dark; they know what they're doing."

"Okay, when I see a woman named Kayli Aubrette, I will make sure she gets back to the hospital."

As Victor was about to help himself to another cup of coffee, he saw Susan staring at him with an expression of horror on her face. But when he approached, Susan darted out of the motel and into a waiting taxi. Victor jumped in his car and followed the taxi until Susan got out some 20 miles away. He parked his car so she wouldn't see him and followed her into the woods. After almost a mile into the woods, Susan sat and leaned back against a large tree, crying.

Victor softly walked up behind her, put his hand on her shoulder, and held her down so she couldn't move.

Susan screamed in terror, "Let me go, let me go! I don't want to go back to the hospital and die!"

Victor pushed Susan on her back and lay on top of her as she screamed in terror. He placed his hand over her mouth, saying, "Listen to me. I am not going to hurt you or bring you back to the hospital. Now promise me that you're not going to scream when I take my hand away from your mouth."

Susan nodded yes as Victor slowly removed his hand. He gently kissed her lips and asked, "Why would I betray the woman I love?"

"You were talking to Albert and told him that you would turn me in."

"I told Albert that when I saw a woman by the name of Kayli Aubrette, I would turn her in. However, you're Miss Susan Wong. Now promise me that you are not going to run off when I get off of you."

Susan smiled, put her arms around Victor, and asked, "What's the hurry? She then passionately kissed Victor's lips over and over again.

After 5 minutes of Susan's passionately making out with Victor. He stopped her and questioned, "How would you feel if somebody came along and caught us in the middle of making love?"

A wide-eyed Susan stated, "I never thought of that. Thanks."

After Victor stood, she sat and leaned against a huge tree, then questioned, "Are you sure you are not going to turn me over to Albert or those men?"

"I may still be trying to figure out the validity that you're a Sprite in a Mandroid's body. But I believe something happened in that hospital that terrified you, and you are scared witless to go back. Because of you are terrifying fear about you returning to the hospital. I will stand guard over you and protect you with my life if need be." He then gently rubbed her back.

Silence reigned for 10 minutes; he stared at Susan, smiling sweetly. Gently pushed her on her back, passionately kissing her for almost 1/2 an hour. He then questioned, "Now, do you believe me that I am not going to bring you back to the hospital?"

Susan stated as she buttoned her pink blouse, "I always looked at you as a straight-laced type of individual. But after what we just did, I see a fire burning inside of you that I want more of, and yes, I do trust you that you're going to protect me." Susan quickly glanced around, then questioned, "Which way to the car?"

Victor looked at Susan and then stated, "I'm not the one who jumped out of the taxi and ran into the woods. Just kidding. We'd go west for about a mile." Victor put his arm around Susan's waist and slowly walked back to the car with her.

At the car, they saw Albert sitting on the hood, who slid off and said, "Thank you for returning Kayli to me."

Susan pounded Victor's chest, screeching, "All the while, you were being nice to me. You were keeping me off guard so you could hand me over to him."

Victor held a hysterical Susan in his arms, then questioned, "Ruth, I'm new at this Mandroid thing. How are the doctors going to fix the problem when Kayli's body has already been cremated and buried? Put her brain in a glass jar, then set it on a shelf in a lab somewhere?"

Albert stated calmly, "There is a woman in a hospital desperately needing that mandroid body. The doctor told me that they would keep Kayli's brain alive until sometime in the future they would be able to take care of her."

"Bear with me for a moment. A twenty-eight-inch tall, 25-year-old Sprite Kayli Aubrette worked on the Sprite security at the OSF. She could fly wherever she wanted, playing stupid games like Tree Dodging, Boulder Racing, and Belly Skimming. She went to the hospital because of an accident, and then the doctors came along and put her brain in a human body, ripping away all the freedom she had. What does Kayli have now? The emotional shock that her wings are gone, and she is in a body twice the size she is used to be in. Many times in the middle of the night, I've had to comfort her because of the emotional trauma. Now you come along and tell her life as she knows it will cease."

"I am sorry Kayli had to go through all that, but there is a thirty-year-old woman in desperate need of that Mandroid body, and I am here to make sure she gets it. Now hand over Kayli."

17

The trip

Victor took a knife from his side pocket, held Susan's left hand, and made a three-inch long cut. Showed Albert the bloody slice and asked, "How many robots do you know that can bleed?"

Albert stared at the bloody wound in shock, then stated, "I guess they gave me the wrong picture." Then walked away confused.

After Albert was gone, a befuddled Susan questioned, "But how?"

Victor took a Kleenex from his side pocket, wiped the blood off of Susan's hand with a smile, and then stated, "It's a trick knife. There's a vial of blood inside the handle of the knife and a little tube that runs down inside the blade, so when I cut, the blood oozes out of the blade to make it look like a wound."

An hour later, Victor parked his car on East Sloan Street, Catawba Island, Ohio, pointed to a small beach, and asked, "You wanna go for a swim?"

Susan took the blanket from the back seat, covered herself with it, and said, "No peaking." Then ducked under the blanket, coming out a little over three minutes wearing a red string bikini. Got out of the car and ran into the water where she splashed around for over two hours.

Later, Susan sat on the blanket to relax when a woman in her late thirties, clad in a Paisley one-piece bathing suit, slowly and carefully approached Susan, studied her for a minute, and then asked, "Why isn't your skin white and wrinkly? You were in that water for over two hours, and you looked like you were never in the water at all. Why?"

"My skin happens to be a little bit more resilient to water than others."

"That the bald-faced lies," stated the woman, "Now, who are you, or should I say what are you?"

"I'm a woman just like you. I have a shapely body that has boobs, and of course, my butt isn't as big as yours, but I'm 100% human. Just because my skin is resilient to water doesn't mean I'm some weirdo. Lady, take a little advice from me and stop watching all those science fiction movies."

The woman screamed, "Liar!" and hit Susan with a baseball bat. Susan raised her right arm to protect herself, but the force of the blow pushed Susan's arm backward, disconnecting it from her body. The woman screamed in horror as she saw the appendage fall to the ground, then hammered Susan's side, ripping the artificial flesh from her body, sending Everybody fleeing in terror.

Victor yanked the baseball bat out of the woman's hand and was about to hit her when a three-foot-tall man with green pants approached. Held up his hands, saying, "Hold on there, lady, that's not the way to handle things. Oh, I'm Patrick Seamus, Fionn, Oisin Colm'O, Donnagái O'Brien, but you can call me Patrick."

"Y, you are a Leprechaun."

"You noticed; let's save the pleasantries for later. Help me get this lassie in me home, which is just over there."

Inside Patrick's rented house, he lay Susan on a stainless steel table in his basement, removed her bathing suit, and examined her to determine how badly she was hurt. He gazed up at Victor and questioned, "Where did you come across this Mandroid, and how long have you been with her?"

"I met her on a ski lift in Vermont several months ago. She's been telling me she's a Mandroid, but I never believed her because her skin is so soft and warm."

"Do you know who she really is?"

"She claims to be Kayli Aubrette, a feisty 25-year-old, twenty-eight-inch tall Sprite from the Planet Pylee who is part of the security at the OSF when she had an accident that put her in the hospital. How bad is she?"

"That hysterical woman did a pretty good job on her. Her right arm is off, which I have; the skin on her right side, from her chest down to her hip, is pretty badly torn, and she is missing her right breast. I don't know why she's offline, but there could be some damage to the cranium. I'll know more once I look inside."

"I'll go back to the beach and see if I can find her boob." Stated Victor.

On the beach, Victor was brushing the sand off of Susan's right breast when the woman who beat her walked up to him with her head down and said, "I am so sorry for damaging that robot. Is it going to be alright? Is there anything I can do to help? Oh, my name is Sally Evans."

Victor brought Sally to Patrick's basement, and she gasped in shock when she saw a badly beaten Susan lying on the table. She rushed to her side, held her right hand, looked at Patrick, and questioned, "Can I talk to her?"

"Yes, you can."

"A mournful Sally looked into Susan's eyes, saying, "I am so sorry I did this to you. Please, please forgive me."

Susan smiled and then slowly nodded her head yes.

Patrick stated, "Everybody out. I've got a lot of work to do on this Mandroid. If you go upstairs, my wife will fix you two a glass of cold lemonade."

Victor and Sally entered an Irish-style living room and sat on the couch; a petite 4'7" tall woman, around 30 years old, with bright red hair done up in a pixie, entered the room. Smiled, saying, "I'm Alexis O'Brian. Can I get you two something to drink?"

"A glass of green iced tea would be great," stated Victor.

Some 6 minutes later, Alexis handed Sally and Victor a frosted glass of green mint iced tea and a plate of glazed doughnuts. She then questioned, "Are you two married?"

Sally quickly answered, "No, we're not. I just came by to see how that robot is doing?"

"You mean the Mandroid. If my Patrick is working on it, you can be guaranteed that it will be in great shape in no time. May I ask if you know who the Mandroid is?"

An inquisitive Sally asked, "What is a Mandroid? I've never heard anything like that?"

"A Mandroid is similar to an Android; only a Mandroid has a human brain inside its skull. Some people have artificial arms and legs, and there are a few people who have artificial bodies."

Sally politely nodded and smiled as if she understood what Alexis was talking about. She stated, "If there is anything I can do to help with that robot Mandroid, please let me know, and I'll be more than happy to help."

Victor took a swallow of his green mint iced tea, then stated, "I think the brain inside that Mandroid belongs to Kayli Aubrette."

Alexa put her hand to her mouth, gasped, and then questioned, "What happened to that sweet Kayli that she needed to have a Mandroid body? The last time I heard, she was in perfect health."

"Kayli was working for the OSF when she had an accident and was sent to the hospital. At the same time, there was a woman who was sent to the hospital in serious condition to have her brain put in a Mandroid's body. But something went wrong, and the woman received Kayli's leg brace, and Kayli's brain was put into the Mandroid. Now the hospital is trying to get Kayly back so they can give Kayli's Mandrake to the woman and put her brain in a jar until they know what to do with her."

"Not gonna happen," stated Alexis. She stared at Sally and then said, "Oh yeah, you're the woman who beat the crap out of Kayli a while ago. Honey, I think you should lay off playing those violent games in virtual reality because it's beginning to affect you?"

"I already said I was sorry. What more do you want?" snapped Sally.

"Every Saturday at six in the evening, my husband holds a Bible study, and you're welcome to join us."

A short time later, Patrick walked into the living room with his head down and said, "I fixed Susan's skin and breast, so you can't even tell it was torn. Her artificial heart and lungs are working fine, but Susan is not responding. I don't know if the connection to her voice and muscles was damaged. So I put her on my cot in the corner of the basement, and all we can do now is wait and pray."

Victor asked, "Can I have some time alone with Susan."

"Sure. What do you have in mind?" asked Patrick.

"I think Susan has all but given up and I may be able to get her to respond.

In the basement, Victor approached the cot, knelt by it, and stated, "Patrick says you're gonna be fine." He pulled back the covers and stared at Susan's nude body for the first time, covered her, went upstairs, and asked Alexis, "Would you happen to have some type of sleepwear that I can put on, Susan?"

Alexis gave Victor a pretty rose-patterned flannel nightgown. He went into the basement and put it on her. Then, he pulled the covers up and made her comfortable. He kissed her lips and said, "Please don't give up; that woman didn't mean to hurt you the way she did." He then rolled Susan onto her side, lifted the back of her nightgown, and gently massaged her back for almost an hour. He stared at her bare bottom, then said, "Do you know you have a nasty mole on your left butt cheek."

"I do not, and stop looking at my derriere," stated Susan as she quickly pulled down her nightgown and sat on the side of the cot.

A joyful Victor quickly threw his arms around Susan, gave her a long kiss, and then said, "Welcome back, my Sweet,"

She gently pushed him away and asked, "What do you mean I have an ugly mole on my derriere?"

"There is a round black spot on your butt. Here, I'll show you."

Susan lifted her nightgown, and Victor gave her a hand mirror. She smiled, saying, "Son of a gun. You're right. I do have a mole on my butt." She quickly looked at Victor with her nightgown up. Smiled, she let go of her nightgown and said, "It's alright if you saw things because we're besties. But let's not make a habit of it because it may lead to sex, which is something we need to stay away from."

Victor stared at Susan, gently put his arms around her, and held her close, saying, "Please forgive me for not believing you when you told me you were a Sprite."

"Sure, no problem. But there's something I need you to do for me."

"What's that," questioned a curious Victor.

"My artificial skin was torn up pretty bad, so I need you to check me to see if I have any scars." And took off her nightgown.

Victor carefully examined Susan's entire torso with his hands for a good seven minutes. He then stated, "You're good to look at. I can't see any scars or marks anywhere on your body. I pushed and pulled everywhere I could, and your skin is intact and will not tear or come apart, but you already knew that didn't you."

Susan silently smiled, then said, "We've been besties for several months, and during those times, you've always kept the two-foot rule which I think sucks big time. So, in a roundabout way, I had you fondle me for attention, and I loved every minute of it."

"In other words, you want me to be a little more physical in our relationship."

"Yes, caressing my face, stroking my hair, scratching between my shoulder blades, and whatever. But stay away from handling my boobies. Oh, before you help me get dressed, could you scratch the itch between my shoulder blades? Oh yes, thank you. Oh, and I'm gonna need you to hook my bra for me."

Once Susan was dressed, Victor stated, "You're a Mandroid, and they don't have itches anywhere, nor do they have tense muscles. So why do you have me give you a body rub?"

Susan grinned and asked, "Do you really want me to answer that question?"

"It's your way of getting attention from me, and that's why you had me check your body for scars and other things, which is why you wanted me to give you a back rub earlier. I promise I'll pay more attention to you. Hey, how about taking a trip to the Philippines to give you time to recuperate from your ordeal? What do you think?"

Susan perked up with excitement at the prospect of traveling and said, "The Philippines sound amazing! I've heard they have beautiful beaches, rich culture, and delicious cuisine. When do you plan on going?"

"Before we leave, did it offend you with the way I rubbed and inspected your body for scars and things like that,"

Susan wrapped her arms around Victor's neck and pulled him close. Her voice lowered, filled with sincerity, and said, "My love, your attention and affection towards me never offend me. Instead, it fills my heart with joy and deepens my love for you."

Later, Victor and Susan stepped off the plane and felt the warm tropical air envelop them. Susan glanced around in wonder, taking in the lush greenery and vibrant colors surrounding them, saying, "This place is absolutely breathtaking. I can't wait to dive deeper into its natural beauty and rich culture."

"Where do you want to go first?"

Susan's eyes twinkled with excitement as she considered the many options, then said, "Well, how about we start by exploring the nearby islands and coves? We could take a boat tour and discover hidden beaches, secret lagoons, and pristine reefs teeming with marine life. Afterward, we can indulge in authentic Filipino cuisine and immerse ourselves in the local traditions and customs."

Victor stated, "With a bright smile, extending his hand towards Susan, inviting her to join him on an exciting journey. Their footsteps echoed against the polished floors of the terminal, as they walked through the creating a melody of anticipation and wonder. As they reached the taxi stand, Victor turned to Susan with an expectant sparkle in her eyes and asked, "Which island shall we visit first, my love?"

"How about the lower part of this island, El Nido?"

"Lower El Nido is known for its secluded beaches, crystal-clear waters, and towering limestone cliffs." Stated Susan.

Victor pointed towards the direction of the town, eager to embark on this new adventure, and said, "Okay, let's head towards Lower El Nido; I can't wait to see what treasures await us there."

18

A time of rest

At the lower part of El Nido Island, Victor asked, "Susan, do you want to swim on a private beach first?"

The thought of having a private beach all to themselves made Susan's heart fluttered with excitement. She gazed out at the sparkling turquoise sea, imagining the tranquil serenity of the water lapping against the shore, then said, "Yes, let's go for it; I can hardly contain my anticipation!"

Victor asked, "Did you bring your one-piece bathing suit or that cute little thing that covers what's needed."

Susan giggled at Victor's playful suggestion and patted her bag, saying reassuringly, "I made sure to bring both, my Love. I want to be fully prepared for whatever adventures await us at the beach."

On a private white sandy beach with the waves crashing on the shore, Victor put down their powder blue blanket and a red cooler full of food. Susan closed her eyes and stretched out her arms, saying, "Victor, we found our own slice of paradise, a secluded stretch of white sand lapped by crystal-clear waves. With the scent of coconut and salt in the air, she helped Victor set up their private oasis, arranging the powder blue blanket and unpacking the tantalizing treats from the red cooler.

Victor asked, "You want to take a dip before we eat?"

"Of course!" stated Susan, eagerly pulling off her clothes, revealing her petite frame clad only in a matching red bikini. She raced towards the water, relishing the feeling of the cool ocean water enveloping her. The two splashed and swam in the cool, clear water for almost 20 minutes. Victor said, "Oh, Sweet, my Love, you lost the bottom half of your bathing suit."

Susan laughed lightheartedly, realizing the predicament she found herself in. Then she said, "Well, I guess it's better off lost than worn!" she emerged from the water and stood proudly before Victor, her slender legs and toned figure on full display in her red bikini top for him to see.

Victor stared at Susan, smiling at him, and stated, "Forget it. Let's go skinny-dipping,"

Susan raised an eyebrow as a mischievous glint formed in her eyes and said, "Are you sure you're ready for that level of commitment?" Susan playfully teased, knowing full well that once they started skinny-dipping, there was no turning back.

Victor smiled and stated, "I like seeing your beautiful bare body."

Susan gave a coy smile and said, "Alright then, if you insist." she slowly undressed, revealing her smooth, toned skin to the warm night air. Her heart raced with nervousness and excitement as she waded into the water, feeling the cool liquid embracing her.

Almost an hour later, they walked to the blanket, hand in hand. Victor gave Susan a beach towel and said, "You were a little nervous about running around naked outside. I understand, and I believe it's a time we'll remember for a long while,"

A sense of contentment washed over Susan as she wrapped herself in the soft, warm blue towel, with the memories of their shared skinny-dipping experience lingering like a sweet, intoxicating fragrance in her mind. Then said, "I think it's safe to say we both enjoyed our little adventure,"

Victor smiled as he wrapped his towel around him and asked, "Was this the first time you went swimming in the nude? Boy, was it fun, and it's something we will remember for a long time because it was the first time I went skinny dipping."

Susan chuckled softly and said, "It was my first time, too. I'm glad we could share this special moment together. It's definitely a memory to cherish."

Victor stated, "It's time to eat." And handed Susan 6 inch long tuna fish sub with cheese onions and tomatoes."

Susan gave a playful grin and enjoyed her food."

After, they gathered their belongings, and packed them away neatly in the red cooler, preparing for their next adventure. Gazed at Victor, and asked, "Now that we've bathed in the sun and sea, what's our next move,"

Victor found a nearby fallen tree and asked Susan to sit with him. He wrapped his arms around her and tenderly kissed her lips. Victor's tender kisses left Susan breathless, and she returned his embrace with equal enthusiasm, her hands resting on Victor's chest, feeling the steady rhythm of his heartbeat. The world fell away, leaving only the two enveloped in a blissful bubble of Love and connection.

Some twenty minutes later, Victor stood and fixed his clothes, smiled at Susan's disheveled condition, and said, "That was more than I had expected. Thank you, my Sweet. Now let's head back to the motel and then for dinner."

Susan rose and brushed off the remaining sand from her clothing. A shiver ran through her body as she recalled the passionate moments she shared under the starry night sky. She nestled close to Victor, grateful for this serene oasis where she could escape the chaos of everyday life and revel in Victor's arms.

At the hotel, Victor put their suitcases down and said, "Let's wash up and go out for dinner. You have any particular place you'd like to go, my Love?"

Susan's stomach growled at the mention of dinner, reminding her how hungry she was. She paused momentarily, thinking of all the delicious options available in their surrounding area. Finally, she decided upon a cozy Italian restaurant they passed earlier, promising delectable pasta dishes and a romantic ambiance. Then said, "How about that quaint Italian spot we saw earlier?"

"A cozy Italian restaurant sounds excellent." stated Victor as he handed Susan her purse and said, "Don't forget this."

Susan took her small purse with a smile, appreciative of Victor's attention to detail. Thanks, Victor." Susan slid the strap over her shoulder, adjusting its position as they stepped out of the hotel room. They enter the dimly lit establishment with its warm and inviting ambiance enveloping them like a comfortable embrace. The sweet aroma of garlic, tomato sauce, and fresh basil fills Susan's nostrils, whetting her appetite further.

"This place looks perfect," stated Victor. He studied the menu, pondering what he wanted to eat. He ordered the salmon with mashed potatoes and green beans, then said, "For some reason, all I could think about today was fish."

Susan eagerly scanned the menu, her gaze landing on the mouth-watering pasta dishes. She decided on a classic Spaghetti Bolognese, hoping it lived up to its reputation as one of the most popular options on the menu. Then she ordered, "I'll have the Spaghetti Bolognese, please."

As the food arrived, Victor asked Susan, "Could you say grace over the meal?"

Susan bowed her head slightly and closed her eyes to offer a heartfelt prayer of gratitude for the food before them and the Love they shared. Her words were soft, spoken with sincerity and reverence, a moment of connection between them and the Saviour.

After a fabulous meal, Victor asked, "Susan, do you want to go back to the hotel?"

Feeling content and satisfied after the delicious meal, Susan nodded in agreement with a smile, "Yes, let's head back to the hotel."

At the hotel, Victor showered off the sand, wrapped a towel around him, crawled into bed without putting anything on, and fell asleep.

Susan stared at Victor, sound asleep, thinking, "I shouldn't do it. But I am too tired to go to my own room. She slipped off her clothes, letting out a gentle sigh of relaxation as she settled into the soft sheets beside Victor for the first time, snuggling close to his side, feeling the warmth of his presence and the comfort of being wrapped in his arms. Then, in the morning, Susan entered into intimacy with Victor for the first time.

After a week of fabulous restaurants, exploring dark caves, and climbing high cliffs. Victor gazed at Susan, relaxing in a chair in her pink step-ins in their hotel room. And asked, "What do you want to do now, my Sweet? I think we've seen it all."

Susan's eyes met Victor's, filled with a mix of exhaustion and satisfaction. Took a deep breath, letting the tranquility of the moment wash over her. She leaned back in her chair, gazing up at Victor with a hint of mischief in her eyes, and said, "Well, my Love, since we've accomplished our bucket list, why don't we create some new memories?"

Victor crawled into bed in his briefs and said, "Let's cuddle and see where it goes."

Susan snuggled into the warmth of Victor's body, feeling his gentle touch against her skin. Her heart beat faster as she sensed a spark of intimacy growing between them. She whispered softly, above the quiet of the room. "Wherever it goes, I'm game."

Victor rolled over in bed the following morning, kissed Susan's luscious red lips, and said, "Our time of intimacy last night was something to remember. Thank you, my Sweet. Now, let us get some rest so we won't fall asleep on the airplane back.

Susan stated, "Your gentle touch and loving words still linger on my skin, filling me with warmth and happiness. I appreciate your affection, dear, so let's get some much-needed sleep."

Upon returning to the US, Victor brought Susan to his log cabin in the back woods of Wisconsin and said, "Would you mind living here? You can have the back bedroom it's complete with a bath,"

An elated Susan stated with a broad smile, "I think it's great. This way, we don't have to keep running from people who want to kill me."

"I'm glad you like the place. Why don't you get acquainted with the cabin and everything? I'm going down to the lake and see if I can catch some trout for dinner tonight." He Gave Susan a kiss on her lips, picked up his fishing rod, and walked to the lake.

Sitting on a large boulder that jutted into the water, Victor patiently waited for a trout to take his bait. A short woman about three feet tall clad in hot pants and a white short-sleeved loose-fitting blouse crawled up on the rock and sat next to Victor. He glanced at her and said afternoon, ma'am, or is it little girl?"

That's Miss because I'm 25 years old, not some old woman with white hair, and the name is Miss Kayli Aubrette to you."

Victor almost dropped his pole when she told him her full name. He maintained his composure, smiled, and then asked jokingly, "You wouldn't happen to work for the OSF on security."

"As a matter of fact, I do, and you would be surprised it's some of the stuff this little Sprite has seen."

Victor slowly turned his head towards Kayli and stated, "You're a Sprite. You wouldn't happen to be from the planet Pylee, and you used to work for Thor the Galaxy Sentinel at the institute?"

"Yes, how did you know?"

"How are you at Tree Dodging and Boulder Racing? Slam into any ducks while Belly Skimming?"

Kayli stood, got in Victor's face, and said, "You can tell, my boss, that I am not coming back to work until he fixes certain safety hazards around the OSF."

Victor stared at Kayli, chuckled, and then stated, "For a moment there, little girl, you almost had me convinced that you are some Sprite from a distant planet. Did Susan put you up to this little charade? You can go back to my cabin and tell her that it almost worked, but you have to get up pretty early in the morning to fool Old Victor."

An incented Kayli stamped her right foot on the rock, hollering, "I am not a little girl! I am a full-grown Sprite!"

"Okay, you're a lady Pixie. Now run along and play in the sandbox or something, and leave me alone so I can catch my dinner."

Kayli quickly slipped out of her clothes, showed Victor her scanty two-piece bathing suit, and questioned, "Do little girls have breasts as big as mine and wings?"

"Ah, no."

Kayli dove into the water, caught a 12-lb trout, threw it on the rock, and said, "There's your dinner, and no, the top of my bathing suit is not stuffed with tissue paper to make me look buxom."

"I can see that." Victor had Kayli turn around so he could examine her wings. He then stated, "Your wings are real. You have the body of a 25-year-old woman, so I guess you must be telling the truth. One more thing, would you mind if I rub my hands over your legs and body? I want to make sure that skin and everything is you and not some fancy makeup garb."

Some five minutes later, an embarrassed Kayli grimaced and asked, "Now that you've had your fun groping and fondling me. Are you satisfied that I am who I say I am?"

"Yes, I am satisfied that you are who you say you are. However, I know of someone who says that she is Kayli Aubrette and has all your qualifications."

"She's an imposter!" Shouted and angry Kayli.

Victor asked, "How do I know you're the imposter and the Kayli I know is the real one."

"Okay, this is something only I know; I was doing my normal rounds at the Omega Flight Squadron Headquarters. Flying around buildings, making sure there were no spies. I then flew through the jungle in a radius around the base to make sure that everything was secure. When I heard giggling coming from a cave. I quietly flew in, and there was a human man fooling around sexually with Sprite Tina. I knew what they were doing because neither one of them was dressed. As far as I was concerned, the man was forcing himself on that poor little thing. But later on, Sprite Tina took me aside and asked me not to say anything, so I never put it in my report, and yes, I know who he was."

"Ohh yeah, assume if I contacted Sprite Tina, she would verify your story."

"You can use my computer watch and give her a call. In fact, I'll give you her address, and you can go there in person and talk to little Tina. She will verify what happened in that cave and who I am."

Victor said, "Oh, I'm sure Tina will verify your story. However, Tina is most likely on the other side of the Galaxy and cannot be reached. Talk to you later. Bye."

A thirty-five-inch tall female midget, dressed in a skimpy bright yellow blouse and jean slacks, approached Victor and said, "I heard you mentioned my name concerning some type of information. I'm Tina. What do you want to know?"

"I'M Victor Wordly. Pleased to meet you."

A shocked Tina asked, "Aren't you the new head of the OSF?"

"Yes, I am; I was appointed by the Galaxy Sentinel himself."

"What are you doing on this side of the Galaxy when you're supposed to be running the Omega Strike Force?"

"I told Thor I would take a sabbatical and get my head in order before I reported for work. That's when I met a lovely young woman by the name of Susan Wong, who seemed to be having a lot of emotional problems and really doesn't know who she is. She says she's Kayli Aubrette, who was accidentally put in a Mandroid's body. I was going to leave her thinking she was some type of a dingbat, but the body she is in is a Mandroid;

who the woman inside the Mandroid is, I don't know. I told the Galaxy Sentinel, and he told me to stay with her and get to the bottom of things."

Victor stared at the heart pendant around Tina's neck and questioned, "I see you're wearing one of the new pendants designed to hide Sprite wings. How are they working?"

"Great, sir. Now, what do you want to know?"

19

The Truth revealed

"I was just talking to a Sprite who calls herself Kayli Aubrette. She told me that you would verify a story about you in a cave with a man, which would prove that the Kayli Aubrette I spoke to earlier is the real one."

"Oh yeah, the story of Sentinel-One and me. We were in the jungle north of Omega Strike Force Headquarters when I was struck by a blast of energy that sent me tumbling down into a thorn bush. Then, was wrapped up in a snake and would have died if it weren't for the quick action of Sentinel One. We took shelter in a cave, and that's when I found out I had a dislocated wing, along with multiple cuts and bruises all over my body, as well as a wounded shoulder from the energy blast. I felt uncomfortable about Sentinel-One tending to my injuries and reluctantly stated, I'm ready to be naked as long as you're gonna help me get better, but watch where you put your hands. After Sentinel One patched up all my cuts and bruises, my dislocated wing was back in place. Sentinel-One couldn't dress me because of the seriousness of my injury so he crawled in the sleeping bag bare chested, lay on his side, and held a shivering me against him, praying the heat from his bare body would keep me from going into shock. In the morning, Sentinel One asked me if I was alright. I told him that I was hurting really bad. So we cuddled in his sleeping bag until I was feeling better. Somewhere around mid-morning, I was feeling good, but I got a little kittenish with Sentinel-One. While we were fooling around in the sleeping bags, he asked if I was sure I wanted to mate with him because he was much bigger than me. I told him that I wanted him more than he knew. So Sentinel One and I entered a mating ritual that would make him my husband or mate. In other words, we had sex. Just as we finished copulating, I saw Kaily at the cave entrance, watching us. She thought that Sentinel One had forced himself on me and gave him a good tongue lashing. Later that day, I caught up with Kayli and told her not to say anything about what happened between me and Sentinel-One in the Cave; yes, Sentinel-One and I are still a couple."

"That confirms the Sprite I talked to earlier was the real Kayli Aubrette, and your ID confirms that you are the real Tina."

"What are you going to do about the impostor?"

"Stay with her because she is in some type of trouble, and I need to find out what kind of trouble so I can help her."

Back at the cabin, Victor cleaned the fish, and Susan baked it for supper along with mashed potatoes and corn. Later that evening, while sitting on the veranda, Victor asked Susan, "How are you sleeping at night?"

"Good, I had a dream last night that I was trapped in a dark room and couldn't get out."

"It had something to do with the fact that you feel trapped in that Mandroid body,"

"That's most likely it," stated Susan as she bent over to pick up a napkin. Victor tackled Susan to the porch floor just as an arrow embedded in the seat behind her. He took his 44 Magnum from his back belt and slowly scanned the wooded area for the slightest movement but saw nothing. Susan stood saying, "Don't be so jumpy, Sweetheart. It was probably a hunter's stray arrow."

Just then, Susan screamed as an arrow struck her right shoulder, causing her to collapse on the porch. Victor fired three shots where he thought the sniper was; he then whispered, "Lie still and pretend that you're seriously wounded." Victor then crawled off the porch, crouched down, and waited for the sniper to make his move.

A tall, lanky woman dressed in black slowly crept up to Susan and pointed her crossbow at her heart to kill her. Victor put his pistol to her head, saying, "Drop the bow, or I'll drop you. Try to escape, and you'll be dead before you take two steps."

Susan rose to her feet, took the bow from the sniper, pulled the arrow out of her shoulder, and then shoved the sniper down in a wooden chair.

Victor pointed his Magnum at the woman's head and asked, "Who are you, and why do you want to kill Susan?"

"Alex told me that Susan Wong had to die because of the secrets she has locked up in that brain of hers."

"What secret?" shouted Victor.

"Susan knows too much." Stated the sniper as a bullet struck her chest, silencing her.

Victor hollered, "Dang, she died before telling us who wanted her dead." He then heard bushes rustling and footsteps as if somebody was running away. He ripped open the woman's blouse and held a napkin to the wound, saying in a soft voice. "Susan, she's barely alive; keep pressure on the wound, and I'll call for help."

Victor made a call on his watch and said, "Thor, this is Victor; I have a badly wounded sniper who tried to kill Susan. All I could get out of her was that Susan knows too much."

A nine-foot-diameter two-dimensional oval appeared ten feet behind Susan. Two men dressed in white quickly floated a white Gurney through it, put the wounded woman on it, and then vanished into the portal. Victor brought Susan inside, took off her top, and used something that resembled an electric razor to heal the wound on her shoulder. Susan put her hand on the healed injury, looked at Victor, and asked, "Who are you?"

"I'm the one who loves and protects you."

"I know that. What I am saying is you're not from this planet."

"Neither are you,"

"What do you mean I'm not from this planet?"

"For one, you call Breakfast the morning meal and so on. You call your bottom your sit-down, which tells me you are a Sprite. So be honest with me. You say you are Sprite Kayli Aubrette, who worked for the OSF, but do you know a Sprite Tina and a Sentinel-One?"

"I don't know, my head is in such a fog and a tailspin because I'm in this Mandroid and it's hard to think straight."

"I pray you find some time to relax, my Sweet."

"I'm trying to but to no avail." Stated a frustrated Susan.

"Why don't you put on your bathing suit and relax by the lake with a mug of coffee,"

"Sounds perfect! I'd love to spend some quality time with you."

Down by the lake, Victor took a swallow of his coffee, glanced at Susan in her red bikini, and then gave her a mug of coffee.

"Aw, thank you, Love. You make me feel like a million bucks the way you take care of me," said a shy Susan.

"You look like a million in that bathing suit of yours."

Susan blushed, then said, "Oh, stop it, you're making me feel embarrassed!"

Suddenly, a portal opened ten feet in front of Susan. She screamed, "Oh God no!" dropped her coffee, and raced into the woods.

Patrick exited the portal, glanced at Victor and then at a fleeing Susan, and asked, "What just happened?"

"I don't know," stated a puzzled Victor, standing to his feet.

"Let's go find her," stated Patrick.

Some two hours later, Patrick pointed to a large Pine tree and stated in a low voice, "She's up there."

Victor stood at the base of the tree, looked up, and said, "It's alright, Sweet. You can come down. It was Patrick who came out of the portal."

Susan climbed down and put her arms around Victor, saying, "I thought some men were gonna come out of that portal thing and drag me off and beat me again."

"Do you know who those men were?"

"No, I don't."

Patrick approached Susan and said, "I need to speak to you for a moment. Is it alright with you, Victor?"

Patrick walked twenty-two feet, had Susan sit on the ground, and talked to her for a half hour. He gave Susan a cup of coffee produced by his digital watch. He approached Victor and stated, "Susan is definitely a Sprite. I could tell by the way she spoke to me and her mannerisms. But who is locked up inside that confused and scared brain of hers, I don't know?"

A short time later, Victor watched Susan playing with some twigs on the ground and asked Patrick, "Why is she acting like a child,"

"Sprites are simple minded foke and have a hard time handling stress."

"Ah, I see. That's why they play games like Tree-Dodging; it helps them cope with things. Since Susan doesn't have her wings, she is in a world of hurt."

"What you need to do is find a substitute for the Sprite games. Prayerfully, that will unlock her mind."

"How do you know so much about Sprites?"

"I was engaged to Sprite Mary-Bell for a few years."

Victor chuckled and said, "Mary-Bell got herself into more trouble than twelve Sprites combined. I remember when she was Belly Skimming. She flew low, so her belly skimmed the water. Broadsided, a duck, and flew end over end and wound up on the beach with a mouthful of sand. Then, there was a time when Mary Bell went Tree Dodging for the first time. She flew in and out and around the trees, zipping and hoping to be number one. She zigged when she should have zagged and flew through a bush with a beast's nest. Poor Mary Bell was laid up for about a week with about a dozen bee stings. But a spunky little lady got up a week later, tried Rock Racing, and almost got herself smushed."

Patrick laughed and said, "I lost track of the number of times Mary Bell flew through a flock of birds, did a face plant in the grass or into a bush, and then complained stupid birds got in my flight path. However, everybody thought it was going to be a disaster when she married and had a baby girl. But Mary Bell wound up to be a model mother and wife, and she straightened out and stopped being a clutch."

"Thanks for dropping by Patrick. But I think it's time Susan and I headed home."

Victor approached Susan and asked, "What would you think about us traveling through space?"

"I've always been fascinated about space travel and wondered what was beyond our solar system."

"Just out of curiosity, how would you feel if we had to get in our star car and fly to the other side of the Galaxy to escape someone who was trying to kill us?"

"Now, that would be one exciting adventure to actually explore the galaxy with you."

Just then, Albert approached Susan, grabbed her left arm, saying, "You're coming with me back to the hospital."

Victor stuck his 44 Magnum in Albert's face, saying, "Let go of Susan, or I'll blow your head off."

"You don't have the guts to shoot an unarmed man. Now put that piece shooter away because I'm taking Susan back to the hospital,"

"Don't you mean you're taking Susan back to Alex so he can bring her through the vortex to Victoria?" Victor paused for a moment, then stated, that's why you're trying to kill Susan because she knows where the vortex is."

Albert ignored Victor's threats as he pulled on Susan's arm. Victor pulled back the hammer on the Magnum, stating, 'I'm warning you, Albert, let go of Susan, or you're a dead man."

"Yeah, like you're gonna kill an unarmed man. Come on, Susan, you're coming with me despite what Vic says."

Albert's lifeless body fell to the ground with a bullet in his head. Susan held on to Victor for comfort and gasped when Albert's body quickly turned to dust and was blown away by a slight breeze.

Victor stated, "We've gotta get out of here before Alex sends more henchmen after you."

An hour later, Susan approached Victor and asked, "All packed. By the way, where are we going?"

In Victor's deep blue SUV, he glanced at Susan in her thin pink halter top and fancy white boxer shorts, then stated, "Computer, bring fusion power online, engage vertical thrusters to full, and retract wheels, then ascend vertically."

Once they were above the treetops, Victor stated, "Susan, hold on to your bloomers because we're out of here."

The SUV shot skyward and was out of Earth's atmosphere in 30 seconds. A wide-eyed Susan said, "Thanks a lot, Vic. Now I have to change my undies. Where are we going?"

"To the Planet Pylee in the Planetary Alliance on the other side of the galaxy. Which should take about an hour."

A shocked Susan said, "The galaxy is over six hundred twenty-one trillion miles across, and you are gonna do it in an hour? Yeah, right."

Susan went into a panic when Victor opened a portal on the dark side of the moon. He brought the star SUV to a halt, put her seat back, lay on top of her, and calmed her down. Susan gazed up at Victor, swiftly threw her arms around him, and kissed him passionately, convincing Victor to get intimate with her.

An hour later, Susan fixed herself and stated, "Ever since Thor put you in charge of the OSF, this little Sprite's been wanting to have sex with you."

Victor stared at Susan for a minute, then stated, "You have your memory back."

"Yes, I do, and that imp who calls herself Kayli Aubrette is an impostor."

"What happened that cleared your head?"

"For the first time since I've been in this mechanical body, I felt real passion while we were mixing it up and remembered where the vortex is."

Victor rubbed Susan's back briskly, saying, "Time to get things done."

As soon as Victor and Susan stepped on the tarmac at the Omega Strike Force Headquarters, Sprite Kayli Aubrette flew up to Susan and bellowed, "Security, to the tarmac on the double, we have an intruder!"

Within seconds, 15 sprites quickly surrounded Susan with their weapons drawn. Kayli pointed to Susan, saying, "When I give the order, kill that miserable piece of work."

Victor stood in front of Susan, gazed at Kayli, and asked, "Isn't the one in charge of the OSF supposed to give the order to terminate a prisoner?"

"Yes, Sir, he is, but Sam isn't here, so it's up to me to give the order."

Victor stated, "Didn't the Galaxy Sentinel appoint a new head of the OSF?"

"Ah, yes, but he hasn't shown up as yet."

Victor ordered, "Hold Kayli,"

Kayli hollered, "What's the meaning of this? I'm in charge of security, so let me go!"

Victor ripped a thin rubber mask off Kayli's face, revealing an imp with dark red skin. Then, he stated, "You're working for Alex and the evil Queen Victoria." Pointing to Susan, Victor said, "This is the real Kayli Aubrette, and she knows where the vortex to Queen Victoria's lair is."

The scared Imp stated, "I'm Imp Sylvia, and I work for Queen Victoria because she'll kill me if I don't do what she says. So please, when this is over, can I please stay in this realm where I am safe and none of the queen's henchmen will kill me."

Victor said, "Once we're there, we need somebody to guide us to the Queen's castle."

"After you exit the vortex, go right and stay on that dirt road through the town. After you've clear of the town, you'll be on top of the hill, and you will be able to see the Queen's castle in the distance."

Victor stated, "Tina, I see you made it back. Can you take Sylvia to the doctor for her checkup? Then, help her with her orientation because she's going to be staying here."

Victor gave Susan a cape, a broad brimmed hat, and energy rifle and stated, "Lead the way to the vortex. Security, you're with us."

Sprite Tom asked, "How can we take down the castle guards when we're just a bunch of tinies?"

"There's fifteen of us, and we have the element of surprise plus the Will-of-the-wisp army,"

At the Cave north of the OSF Headquarters Susan touched a round rock jutting out of the wall, causing it to fall straight down onto the floor, revealing a mass of swirling energy.

Little Sprite Meme stated, "We have to go in that thing! Will be eaten alive."

Victor picked up the trembling Sprite, saying, "You're gonna be fine as long as you stick with me."

Victor and the rest charged into the vortex and found themselves standing in the charred remains of what used to be a green meadow. Tippy stated firmly, "You know what to do. I'll drop everyone off at their appointed destinations, and then we'll take out the guns together."

"Cloaks!" shouted Debbie, "Here comes the reinforcements!"

Skirting around the perimeter of the battle, Gamma scooped her companions up in her arms, then took flight, depositing them two hundred yards from the lightning cannons. Susan quickly leveled here energy rifle at the massive fortress and fired, only to scorch the exterior, "Dang!" screamed Susan, "Now, what am I going to do?" She smiled and commented, "What any woman would do when she's in trouble, use her femininity—glancing up momentarily to watch the Wisp army swoop down towards the castle. Susan quickly covered her ears as the lightning cannon let go of a charge. She knocked on the door, Susan questioned sweetly, "Can anyone in there help me? I seem to be lost." As soon as the door opened, Susan tossed a grenade and dove for cover.

"Oh, Crap," hollered Susan, "The whole installation isn't supposed to explode! Come on, feet, don't fail me now!"

A shock wave threw Susanto the ground as the lightning cannon installation exploded, showering the countryside with debris. Thankful to be alive, Susan stood up, slowly scanned the sky, and sighed as she watched the other lightning cannon blast the Wisp army out of the sky. She tapped her watch and said, "Mission complete. Going after the Queen."

"Stay where you are," ordered Gamma.

"If someone doesn't take out the Queen soon, we're gonna lose this battle. Oh, just FYI, use your feminine charm to gain access, then blow them up. Gotta go."

"Susan, stay there, and that's an order!" Shouted Gamma over the com line.

"Hello. Gamma, You're breaking up. Can you repeat that last statement again? Did you say you're ordering me to take out the Queen? Okay, consider it done."

Susansnickered as she ended the transmission. Spotting a turquoise Wisp lying on the ground nearby, she rushed over to assist.

"I'm alright," groaned the Wisp; we're not used to such a powerful weapon."

"Let me help you up, replied Susan, "Are you sure you're alright? That burn on your chest looks really nasty."

"I'll be fine. You take care of the Queen."

Several hundred yards from the castle gate, Susan activated her camouflage unit in the cloak. Blasting a hole in the wall, she proceeded to the inner courtyard and headed straight for the throne room, then hollered, "Hey, Victoria! It's time to pay the piper!"

The Queen casually strolled from behind a marble column and queried, "Looking for me? Why are you hiding? Afraid?"

Susan turned off the cloak's camouflage of her cape and questioned, "Where is the real Alex?"

"Oh, someplace out of the way. You come here to die? Because that's what you're going to do." The Queen then shouted, "Guards, kill her!"

The throne-room lit up, as a barrage of energy blast bombarded Susan for a minute.

"Missed me," Susan remarked sarcastically.

Victoria gracefully strolled across the throne room, sat on her gold throne, and stated, "You might as well give up. Because you can't destroy me."

"That's what you think," answered Susan as she placed her energy rifle on her left arm and fired. The wave of yellow energy instantly engulfed the throne, melting it. The Queen sprang to her feet as her skin slowly dripped off her metal body, and she shrieked, "I said, kill her, you bumbling idiots!"

The castle guard's eyes widened in horror as they watched their beloved Queen transform into a robot.

"Where's Alex?" hollered Susan.

He's in the dungeon. I'll get him for you," one of the guards said.

Susan leveled her gaze at the Queen and stated, "It's over, Queeny. She leveled her energy rifle at the robot queen and fired a continuous blast of energy. The robot shrieked and thrashed, trying to escape but Susan kept firing until all that was left was a puddle of molten metal.

"I'll signal the cease fire," stated the guard, "Oh, what do you want to do, with the one they call Alex?"

"Give him to one of the Wisp. They'll know what to do. Now, if you will excuse me, I've got a machine to destroy."

In the tower, deep in thought, Susan stared out the window at the charred field, contacted Gamma, and said, "It's over. The Queen is dead, and Alex is safely on his way home. I need everyone to leave before I destroy the vortex device."

"I thought I told you no heroics, Susan," bellowed Gamma.

"No heroics, Sir. It's the only way. Now, get your butts out of here!"

When the last of the Wisps had vanished through the vortex. Susan leveled her energy rifle at the vortex machine and fired. Sparks and smoke bellowed up as Susan muttered, "Not again! When am I gonna learn." Susan was halfway down the tower stairs when the top of the tower exploded. She camouflaged herself as she quietly walked through the cheering masses back to the charred field. She paused, then waved her arm out in front of her, hoping to locate the vortex and go home. Realizing her fate, Susan returned to the tree hut to plan her future. Finding a pile of clothes in the corner of the hut, Susan packed her Omega uniform in a cloth sack and put on the clothes.

some weeks later, Susan was foraging for food and bumped into a tall, orange figure. "Excuse me, but you're in my way. I need to get that fruit for my dinner."

He smiled at her and said, "Can I help you, Little Miss?"

"Ah, isn't that supposed to be my line?"

"I'm here to bring you home. By the way, my name is Master Ashdothmpisgah Shechaniah Bashanmhavothmjair but you can call me Ab."

"Home? That's a laugh. No on one can do that, mister. I'm stuck in this dimension for the rest of my life."

"Victor sent me here after you so take my hand. It's time to go home."

"Do you mind if I get something first?"

With her sack slung over her shoulder, Ab reached into his bag and took out a foot in diameter emerald, green orb. Held it over his head, and began to glow until it had engulfed them. Seconds later, Susan was standing by the fountain in the Institute's Arboretum.

"Come, there's someone who wants to see you in the cafeteria," stated Ab.

"I am so dead," muttered Susan, "Tippy is going to kick my butt all over this planet for disobeying a direct order."

The hall was lined with well-wishers, all happy to see her back. Victor approached her and silently opened the cafeteria doors. Susan's eyes widened in shock as she whispered, "Mom, Dad. As you can see I'm not a Sprite anymore."

Susan's father stated, "it doesn't matter you're still our daughter."

Her parents rushed to greet her. Her Sprite father proudly boasted, "My big daughter, the hero."

"Mom, Why did you abandon me when I was sick? You don't know how much I cried when you left."

"Your father lost his job; we had no money. When you took ill, the only thing we could do was let the State give you the medical attention we could not afford. We tried to find you later, but they would not give us any information on you. Then, when we heard you were trapped in the vortex, I thought we had lost you for good."

"Ah, Mom, Dad. What are you doing in a top secret, facility?"

"We work here. Your father is head of the research lab; I work in housecleaning. Why?"

"Because I work here, too."

Moe hugged her father, saying, "Dad, hold me." Susan let go, stepped back, and said, "I'm no hero. I disobeyed a direct order. Now, I have to report in to have my butt kicked."

Susan's mother glanced at her husband and commented, "Now, where have I heard that before? I see the apple doesn't fall far from the tree."

Susan stood on a small, white bridge in the Arboretum, staring into a stream, when Victor strolled up to her and stated, "You're looking better."

"Thanks for not throwing the book at me, for disobeying orders."

Epilogue

There was a weeklong celebration for the end of the evil Queen Victoria. Moe stared at Alex, relaxing in a lawn chair, enjoying a tall, frosty glass of lemonade. She slowly approached and stared at him.

Alex stated, "You mind not doing that? You're giving me the creeps, lady."

Moe shouted, "Alex, it's me, Moe, the woman in the wheelchair!" She then yanked him out of his chair and kissed him. Then she asked, "Now, do you remember me?"

"Oh hey, it's great to see you. How have you been?"

"Great, let's go someplace quiet so we can be alone and talk."

During the celebration, Tippy brought Susan into the doctor's office. Then stated, "During the raid on Queen Victoria's realm, we found something you may be interested in." Tippy brought Susan into a white operating room. Pointed to a Gurney saying, "For some strange reason, the queen kept your body alive. All we have to do is transfer your brain back into your body, and you'll be little Sprite Kayli Aubrette once again."

Susan shouted for joy, excited that she was going to be a Sprite again; she then felt a hand rest on her right shoulder. She turned around and stared at Victor with an expression of bewilderment on his face. Susan turned back and stared at her little body lying on the operating table, waiting for her brain. She quickly pulled out the plugs to life support and threw her arms around Victor, saying, "Little Sprite Kayli Aubrette, head of security, is dead. My love, my devotion goes to Victor, who kept me going when everything around me was falling apart." She then kissed him.

Victor stated, "You can always join the OSF,"

"That'll work," stated Susan eagerly.

Printed in the United States
by Baker & Taylor Publisher Services